William Bannatyne

**Poems and Songs on Various Subjects**

William Bannatyne

**Poems and Songs on Various Subjects**

ISBN/EAN: 9783744771344

Printed in Europe, USA, Canada, Australia, Japan

Cover: Foto ©Andreas Hilbeck / pixelio.de

More available books at **www.hansebooks.com**

# POEMS AND SONGS

ON

## VARIOUS SUBJECTS.

BY

## WILLIAM BANNATYNE.

---

" Leeze me on rhyme, it's aye a treasure,
My chief—amaist my only pleasure ;
At hame, a-fiel', at wark or leisure,
      My Muse, kind hizzie.
Tho' rough and raplock be her measure,
      Is seldom lazy."—BURNS.

---

TORONTO:
JAMES CAMPBELL & SON,
1875.

PRESBYTERIAN PRINTING OFFICE, TORONTO.

# PREFACE.

———

THE Author of this volume, in offering it to the public, indulges the fond hope of its being favourably received by the generality of those readers who have already been familiar with his verses; appearing as they have from time to time, in the pages of a variety of our local provincial journals and other periodicals, as well as in several in the United States, to which publications he has for many years been a contributor. Finding that his popularity accorded him a certain ascendency among his contemporary rhymers; he has been induced to make the present effort of appearing in the literary arena in book form; and being (so truly poet-like) as purseless as *that loneliest of all desert birds, the Pelican*, he has adopted the present size, style, and mode of publication.

In order to suit the limits of the work, as well as to avoid all subjects of a directly personal nature, that might prove tantalizing to individual feelings, he has, in consultation with several friends, made a careful selection of pieces, for the most part, in lyrical form, so as to introduce as much variety of sentiment as possible; and, having the elevation of the human intellect always in view, there will be nothing found therein of a harshly grating satirical nature ; nor in any way deleterious to, or at variance with sound moral, and social principles ; whilst the leaden-eyed Dæmen of dulness will be found to wave his shadowy wing with so light an effect, as to preclude all chances of leaving a haggard ghost behind.

To those gentlemen and friends, by whose counsel and assistance he has been enabled to make this offering to the public, he gratefully dedicates the volume ; whilst its contents, whatever their merits may be, he leaves for the tastes and judgments of his readers.

WILLIAM BANNATYNE.

ASHFIELD, ONTARIO,
*May,* 1875.

# CONTENTS.

## PHILOSOPHIC SUBJECTS.

## DIDACTIC AND GENERAL SENTIMENT.

## NATIONAL AND HEROIC SENTIMENT.

## MISCELLANEOUS PIECES—PATHETIC AND HUMOROUS.

# PHILOSOPHIC SUBJECTS.

## IS MIND IMMORTAL?

IS there a world beyond the one
Whereon our mortal course we run,
This sublunary, care-fraught sphere
Of passion, turmoil, vice and fear?
Where fitful Nature's light or shade
Paints but the living and the dead;
This transient round of joy and sorrow,
Where smiles to-day from Hope we borrow,
To point Despair's dark pangs to-morrow?
Here Mind, whate'er its magnitude,
Is but a flower in Spring's weak bud;
A nurseling at the breast of nature,
Unweaned by time, whate'er its stature,
And ne'er can reach perfection's bloom.
If there 's no world beyond the tomb
Where its expanding folds may shed
Fragrance, to endless verdure wed;
Some realm, where life, and light, and bliss,
Live, shine, and charm, unknown to this!
Here virtue seems a desert flower,
And vice, a weed in palace bower;
Here, virtue on the withering blast
Of stern adversity seems cast,
Unshielded on the barren wild,
In blight and bloom alike exiled.

B

Meanwhile, in fortune's golden beams,
Vice lives, and basks, and breathes, and teems,
Big with a load of prosperous years,
Unpierced by want, unstained by tears ;
Till tottering age resigns its load
Of garnished guilt in death's abode.
What merit, then, can virtue have
If being ceases with the grave ?
Or what hath vice itself to fear,
If both have fixed their limit here ?
How vain were wisdom's rules ordained !
How vain are passion's powers restrained !
How vain were honesty and worth !
How vain each talent prized on earth !
How vain affection's every tie !
How vain devotion breathed on high !
How vain were reason's gifts designed,
To charm and cheat a dying mind !
How vain prophetic Hope was given,
To mock us with a visioned heaven !
How vain were all we hear and see,
And think, and feel ourselves to be !
If midst the wreck of death-chill'd fires
Man's intellect with life expires !
But no—a voice beyond the tomb
Bursts through its silence and its gloom ;—
From Calvary's mount o'er every clime
It thrills with cadence more sublime
Than aught e'er charmed the ear of time.
It tells us that oblivion's tide
Can only earth-sprung vapours hide :
That death can only chain our dust :
Mind lives, beyond corruption's rust !
Beam of that cloudless, quenchless light
That shone ere day awoke from night !
Ray of that pure celestial flame
Whence all created radiance came !

Spark of that sun-creating fire
That burns while suns and stars expire.
Immortal mind! destined to be
The tenant of eternity!
Be then my lot the lowly one,
Ne'er fired by false ambition's sun ;
Mine the meek path, where virtue treads
To purer bliss than fortune sheds ;
That Paradise whose dawn-beam throws
A halo round lips direst woes ;
Unlike the retrospective heaven
From fortune sordid votaries riven,
As grasping at fates brink, they fall,
Wrapp'd in doubt's dark cimmerian pall.

## DETRACTION.—AN ODE.

### I.

JUDAS' spirit dark and dire,
Swelled by rancour's foulest fire,
Mystic saws of hellish lore,
Learned thy midnight vigils o'er.
Slanders thousand pointed tongue
Steep'd in malice sharp and strong,
Envy's dagger poison—whetted,
Clogg'd in soul-blood, still unsated,
Shielded 'neath religion's wing,—
Whither art thou journeying?

Thine, the sanctimonious mien ;
Thine, the jaundiced eye of spleen,
Giving colours of its own
Unto all it looks upon ;
Thine, the syren tongue that says

Every thing in virtue's praise;
Like the reptile that doth sing
To the prey it means to sting;
Like the fabled vampyre's art,
Soothing, while it sucks the heart;
Like the Upas' breath that bears
Poison to the subtile airs.
Foster nurse of jealousy
From what carnage dost thou hie?
From what banquet hast thou sped?
On what victim hast thou fed?
Gorged from many a bleeding wound,
Busy demon, whither bound?

## II.

From where'er the winds have birth,
'Neath the sky, and o'er the earth;
From where'er the sunbeams play,
Or the moon omits a ray—
Wheresoever night or day
Hath an ear, or hath an eye,
Round the world, and 'neath the sky!
From where'er is found a tongue
With the nerves of rancour strung
I have been—where have I not?—
At the farm and at the cot;
Thro' the mead, and up the steep,
Where the rustic tends his sheep;
At the parsonage, and in
Other scenes of pious din;
For with devotion I am kin.
In the squire's and baron's hall,
In the assembly, at the ball;
And where titled galls get vent
In a mimic parliament.
I have basked in royal smiles

Brightest in the British isles.
I have worn a royal crown;
I have sat on empire's throne.
I have fed on viands good;
Virtue's tears, and groans, and blood,
Warmly gushing from a heart
Gorged by many a hidden dart;
I have left a havoc rare!
Never victim half as fair! *
I am ranked the mightiest one
'Mongst the fiends of Acheron.

## THE AULD CHAPEL GREEN.

O'er the happy scenes o' childhood's years,
　　My fancy loves to pore,
And the sunny joys that filled life's dream,
　　In the sweet days o' yore.
The birds, the butterflies and bees—
　　The meadow and the fell,
Whar I pu'd the modest gowan
　　And the blushing heather-bell.
They be joys I never could forget
　　Wharever I hae been;
The gowden joys o' childhood's years,
　　By yon auld chapel green.

How dear! when rosy May bedeck'd
　　Each landscape far and wide,
And the mountain brows were mirrored
　　In the dreamy breast o' Clyde,
When the blithesome Merle and Thrastle sang,
　　The woodlan' echoes woke,

* Lady Flora Hastings.

And the Cuckoo's welcome cadence rang
    Frae yon auld ivied oak.
Ee'n the auld wa-hauntin' baukie bird,
    I chased sae oft in e'en,
Recalls my thoughts to childhood's years,
    And yon auld chapel green.

Afar o'er ocean's distant waves,
    I've roam'd on foreign strand,
Whar nature pours her choicest stores
    To gem the tyrant's land :
Whar endless summer's gowden smiles
    O'er stream and mountain play,
And every flow'r but freedom springs
    Beneath the partial ray.
But aye, my thoughts and dreams returned
    Amidst each glowing scene,
To revel in life's morning bow'rs
    By yon auld chapel green.

'Tis not that infancy to age
    Such pleasure can impart,
As fills my heart in after years
    Wi' day dreams o' the heart.
But there were spells o' fonder pow'r
    To manhood's feeling dear,
Bright beamy hopes like beacon stars
    Whose haloes pointed here.
Truth's living light that 'lumed life's path,
    Tho' clouds might rise between,
And led my spirit back again
    To yon auld chapel green.

May never ruthless vandal's han'
    Assail that sacred spot,
Where rest in peace, frae age to age,
    The bones o' mony a Scot.

The patroit mind must still revere
   Each ancient hoary fane,
That tells in silent eloquencē
   The tales o' ages gane.
Then leeze me wi' the soothin' thocht
   When death shall close my e'en,
I'll sleep wi' those I lov'd the best,
   Neath yon auld chapel green.

---

## FEAR NOT TO DIE.

FEAR not to die !
   The fleeting vapour breath
Could never prove the patriot's greatest care ;
The traitor, tyrant, coward, shrinks from death ;
The true, the wise, the virtuous ne'er despair.

   Fear not to die !
   If rectitude of heart
Hath borne thee bravely thro' the strifes of time,
If pure integrity hath been thy chart,
And life's affections free from lust and crime.

   Fear not to die !
   The bonds of human love
Are often reft more rudely than by death ;
Ah ! sure when purer spirits plead above,
Man might renounce his doubt to seal his faith.

   Fear not to die !
   The sordid miser quakes,
As prone at Mammon's glittering shrine he kneels :
The upright heart no earthly idol makes,
To it no brooding terrors death reveals.

Fear not to die !
Who art or has't no slave
Yoked in oppression's litter, blood-stained bond ;
Let crouching serf and despot dread the grave ;
The brave, the truly great have joys beyond.

Fear not to die !
Would'st thou on earth be free,
To nature's God thy spirit's homage lend ;
Time is but the threshhold of eternity,
And life begins where mortal sufferings end.

Fear not to die !
And haughtiest human pow'r,
Tho' poised by creed and sword, on loftiest throne,
Will in thy presence awed and crest-fallen cower,
Whilst thou serene, erect, will stoop to none.

Fear not to die !
Inflexible in faith,
Steadfast in principle, in conscience clear,
Sublimely o'er the imputed glooms of death,
Thy soul may soar to its immortal sphere.

## WE ARE NEVER ALONE.

WE are never alone in the journey of life,
   Tho' desert and dreary we oftentimes seem,
We are never alone—our companions are rife ;
   Be they real, ideal, or seen in a dream :—
In varied profusion our pathway is strewn ;
Let us roam when we may, we are never alone.

There never was solitude yet upon earth,
   In its deepest recesses Society rules :

We are links of its chain from the hour of our
        birth,
    And all who esteem themselves hermits are fools :
To tropical desert or far frigid zone,
Let us tread where we will, we are never alone.

There are thousands around us,—the volatile air
    Is pregnant with voices familiar and dear,
Or harshly discordant, or broken by care,
    Or gifted with melodies glowing to hear;
And they speak to our souls about all we have
        known,
They may gladden or grieve, but we are not alone.

Fell envy, and malice, and falsehood, and fear,
    In direful array 'gainst our peace may conspire;
We may claim from the world scarce a sigh or a
        tear,
    And seek from its rudeness afar to retire :
What cavern so tranquil, such solace can own ?
Whilst self remains present, we are not alone.

Old memories, sympathies, fancies and forms,
    Blend former, and present, and future in one ;
We must live in their midst, be they horrors or
        charms,
    In the gloom of despair, or the blaze of hope's
        sun ;
All space teems with being, all silence with tone,
For our bane, or our bliss we are never alone.

We are never alone thro' creation afar,
    The life-giving spirit of nature doth sway,
As full, as supreme, in a stone as a star :—
    Presides o'er all changes, but owns not decay;
Oblivion exists not—no vacuum is known ;
God is present in all,—we are never alone.

All our wanderings He marks, all our joys and
    our woes,
    And all to our vices and virtues allied :—
No secret so deep but His eye can disclose,
    In our crimes, in our errors, our thoughts and
    our pride ;
All is full in His sight—there is nothing unknown,
In life or in death, we are never alone.

## UPWARD AND ONWARD.

Upward and onward forever ;
    That's the true maxim of mind :
Our souls are afloat on life's river,
    To combat with tide and the wind.
Forward ! by skilfully steering,
    The quicksands and reefs we may clear :
Thro' adversity's tempests careering,
    Let us quail not, the slaves of our fear.

Upward and onward, unceasing ;
    That's the true tenor of life :
'Tis no airy phantom we're chasing,
    And why should we lag in the strife ?
Upward ! tho' midway the mountain,
    The scar and the avalanche frown ;
Let our spirits drink freely hope's fountain,
    But never despairing sink down.

Sterner and firmer resolving ;
    That's the true lever of power ;
Remember, life's wheel, while revolving,
    Obstructions may meet every hour ;
What, tho' thrown down by its lumb'ring
    At times, we may grope in the dust ;

Ne'er let vicissitudes cumbering
    Fetter our souls with mistrust.

Discard every cynical notion ;—
    Sophist and cynic are blind ;
'Tis integrity, love, and devotion
    That burnish the axis of mind :
Landward, or seaward, undaunted
    Stem the jagg'd wild, or the wave ;
The heart by weak cowardice haunted,
    Befits but the breast of a slave.

Higher and prouder careering,
    Poised on the pinions of faith,
Like eagles, when danger is nearing,
    Let us soar in defiance of death :
Upward and onward forever,
    Toiling while yet it is day,
Trusting in Providence ever,
    You'll find "with a will there's a way."

## TO A CAGED LARK, ON SETTING IT AT LIBERTY.

WHAT robs thy bosom's peace, what mars thy joy?
All day on restless pinion fluttering round,
And tapping with thy little tender bill
Upon the wiry gratings of thy cage :
I've placed fresh seed within thy well-cleaned crib,
And fill'd thy crystal horn with beverage new ;
A green, soft sod I've placed beneath thee too ;
And giv'n thee moss, and straw, and downy wool,
To nestle in, and be at happy rest !
Still, still incessant fluttering to be free !

And loathing at the good things of this life,
Thou seem'st a peevish, carping malcontent ;
Unlike thy kindred minstrels of the wild,
Who having neither home nor friendly aid
To foster them, beyond their own devoir,
Nor well-ribb'd tenement to guard their lives
From ruthless talons of devouring hawk, .
Yet prone upon the airy summit poised
Of fleecy cloud, make glad the volant air,
With wild sweet rush of rapturous melody !
Whence comes their joyance ? whence thy strong
      disgust ?
Their lays elated, tell of love and bliss !
But thine, the dissonance of dark despair !
Has Nature, in her wide, free field of flight,
Charms more congenial to thy throbbing breast—
Which now thou peck'st—than favoured haunts of
      man ?
Man ! the proud lord of wide creation's range !
Who culls the harvest of each golden field,
Where'er the sun sheds light or earth drinks dew ;
Who spans old ocean with his iron rule,
And chains the lightning to the veriest point,
Subservient to his use !—ah yes ! methinks
In Nature's air I hear thy warm appeal,
In guileless, ardent, strong remonstrance, strike
This touching, strong conviction on my soul :—
" Man ! thou usurper of a right divine ;
" Vain, callous, selfish, arrogant, severe,
" Monopolist of titles and of power ;
" Tyrant, and ingrate to thy being's laws,
" *Who dreadest liberty even in a lark!*
" Whence is thy sovereignty, proud giddy fly,
" That buzzest only thy brief summer day
" In dreamy majesty ?—ambition's sport !
" Whom ? but a passing breath called into being !
" Whom ? but a passing breath as quick destroys !

" Impious imposter ! can thy vaunted rúle
" Avert the simplest law which Nature's God
" Ordained, to guide the circling Universe ?
" The Power that planned the spheres hath also
" Called the lark into existence ! The green earth,
" With its diversity of healthful herbs,
" The roaming clouds that wreath the giant hills,
" The scented zephyrs, and the gleaming dews,
" The home, the food, the atmosphere of song,
" Created as the free-born sphere of life,
" Wherein its lot uncircumscribed should be."
Minstrel of liberty, and sunny love !
Go to thy native element, sweet bird !
Call back the glad sensations of life's morn ;
Sport with the downy clouds ; and cull fresh joy
From healthful atmosphere and flow'ry sod !
Nature hath charms revivifying still :
Tho' thy shorn wings, and cruel prison bars,
Have long restrained the freedom of thy flight,
And chilled the raptures of thy heaven-born strain,
Drink fresh again the fountain of thy life;
And teach frail man the virtue of thy freedom
In songs ; more proud of being thus set free !
So perish bondage whereso'er it reigns !

## STANZAS ON PROVIDENCE.

A SPECIAL kindly providence
  Sits, ever up above,
With eye of steadfast vigilance
  And smile of heavenly love,
It never slumbers night or day ;
  Nor flags with toil o'er wrought,
But guides from errors tempting way
  The mind with virtue fraught.

It never scorns at indigence
  As selfish powers of earth ;
For well it knows, the lust of pride
  Would tread our humble worth ;
The humble mind, the honest aim,
  The truthful heart and tongue,
It warms with inspiration's flame
  And clothes in light and song.

It soars above the furrow'd field
  Where toils the weary hind,
And gently fans his sweaty brow
  With cooling zeyphrs kind ;
It whispers to his soul the charm
  Of home's pure sympathies ;
And strengthens more his brawny arm
  To guard those sacred ties.

Its halo gilds the drapery
  Of summer's tranquil sky ;
Where sings the lark in July's dawn
  Its heaven-tuned rhapsody ;
The shepherd panting up the steep
  In grateful homage kneels
And deems a world's ambition cheap
  To half the joy he feels.

Above the tented battle field
  When duty calls, to save
From rebel ire, or spoiler's brand
  The birthright of the brave ;
It hovers round the soldier's rest
  Bright visions to impart ;
Till many an humble ungemmed breast
  Reveals a hero's heart.

It rides above the bursting spray
  Of ocean's boisterous tides ;

And saves the sailor's trusty ship
   Whilst tempest lash her sides ;
By whirlpool, reef and crested shoal :
   Along life's treacherous main,
It guides him to the hoped for good ;
   And still he trusts again.

O'er feigned friendship's enmities,
   Dark treachery and wrong,
It poises high the ardent soul
   Of each true child of song !
Tho' barr'd on earth from every bliss,
   To baser spirits given,
Triumphant o'er life's wretchedness
   He sings his way to Heaven.

## THE APPROACH OF WINTER.

Now cold November's gurly gale
Comes blustering down the Boreal way,
And Nature, with a rueful mein,
Beholds her sweetest charms decay.
No more the glancing streamlet's hymn,
In happy tinklings cheers the dell ;
Each fitful voice in glen and grove,
Seems sighing out the year's farewell.

No more, on glittering billows borne,
The stately bark in grandeur glides,
But roaring waves, in turbid foam,
Fierce combat wage with Huron's tides ;
No more its banks in leafy pride
Through bowery shades invite to stray ;
No more their sylvan echoes ring
Responsive to the stock-dove's lay.

For Winter, in his threatening ire,
Hath cast abroad his blighting frown,
And scattered all the glowing joys
That gemm'd fair summer's vernal crown;
High piled along the wave-lash'd strand,
He rears his jagged icy wall,
The rampart of his ruthless reign
To hold the gelid floods in thrall.

Far-veiled behind yon murky zone
Of sable clouds, that denser lower,
The pallid sunbeams southward fare,
Too faint to pierce its ebon power.
How wild each sound, how chill each scene
How sad the mind's presaging dread;
How hope recoils, how misery pines!
How penury shrinks with drooping head.

The plumy tribes of grove or lake,
To more congenial scenes have flown;
The reptile to his dormant rest,
The wild beast to his den hath gone;
But whither can misfortunes child,
Evade the woes that round him loom?
What home can shield the outcast's head,
Or guard him from a wretch's doom?

Perchance e'en now the haggard eye
Of famine—grisly tyrant—peers
Where humble worth unfriended groans,
And stayless virtue hides her tears;
Perchance some widow'd victim strains
Her famish'd infants to her breast,
While anguish chills its vital tide,
By sickness, cold and hunger press'd.

Awake ye souls, that wrapp'd in dreams
By fortune's partial bounties given,

Awhile your festial joys refrain,
Nor deem that earth is all a heaven :
Let Sympathy's diviner toils
To want and woe direct your care :
Go soothe the pangs, and dry the tears,
And smooth the brow of wan despair.

## THERE IS NOTHING SO HOLY AS LOVE.

REFLECTING afar on the science of life :
It's duties, affections, and vanities rife ;
    What history may teach, or tradition imply ;
Since the first starry birth of the universe sprung,
And the seraphim choir's raptured melody rang
    Thro' the echoing vault of the sky.
What worth, or what glory, or grandeur displays :
What genius conceives, or what sentiment sways,
    Within, or around, or above :
In the holiest depths of the holiest hearts,
Where the well-spring of virtue its treasures imparts,
    There is nothing so holy as love.

We count on the wonders which science unfolds ;
What the earth, what the air, what the vast ocean
    holds
    In its deep and mysterious cells !
We gaze in mute awe, or we shudder with dread,
At the relics sublime of those ages that sped,
    Long ere aught of man's origin tells !
From structures stupendous, by Tigris, or Nile,
Our reason shrinks back with a fearful recoil,
    And hangs o'er the nest of the dove :
Meet emblem—proverbial of purity's reign !
How free from ambition, and riot's foul stain !
    There is nothing so holy as love.
    C

As we pour o'er the records of history's page;
And the names it transmits us, from age unto age,
   Of the heroes whose deeds have ennobled our
      race :
The warriors who bled in their loved country's
      cause ;
And gloried to die for those rights, and those laws
    Which tyrants had dared to deface :
The patriots brave of the eloquent tongue,
The martyrs that suffer'd, the bards who have sung
    With fervor inspired from above !
Tho' proudly we render the homage they claim ;
And feed our ambition with yearnings for fame,
    There is nothing so holy as love.

Behold when the infant enfolded at rest,
Lies nestling its form in its mother's warm breast,
    And radiantly smiles in its happy repose!
Unconscious of life's looming dangers, it clings
To the fold of her heart, from whose rich welling
      springs
    Its nuturing element flows.
And mark when the cares and the sorrows of years
Assail its first path, in the valley of tears.
    With thorny perplexities wove,
What toil, what devotion, what courage and skill
Directs its young footsteps, to ward them from ill!
    There is nothing so holy as love.

Aloft on the mountains ; away in the vales
Mid the tints of the morn ; and the balm of its
      gales,
    And the chorus that rings from the clouds and
      the brake,
Where glows the fair landscape with forest and mead;
And the flocks gaily sport, or contentedly feed
    On the soft verdant brink of the lake,

The fancy may roam with unsated delight
'Till her vision is veiled by the curtain of night :
   And the song'spirit sleeps in the grove ;
But the shrine of the heart, nought of light can
    divest :
While affection's soft current throbs warm in the
    breast :
   There is nothing so holy as love.

O love !—whatsoever thy form or thy sphere,
Without thee, how rude would creation appear !
   How cold and how dark, and distractedly wild !
What horrible instincts would ravage and waste !
No impulsive benignant—no refuge nor rest :
   No altar of truth undefiled !
Thine all the fair fabric of Nature's vast fold,
From the simplest of forms that have birth in
    earth's mould
   To the heaven of heavens above !
The God of omnipotence bends from his throne ;
And bids us to hallow thy name as his own !
   There is nothing so holy as love.

---

## THE POET'S COMMON LOT.

BROTHER Minstrel sit by me :
I will share this crust with thee,
Tough, and mouldy tho' it prove,
We'll munch it just for kindred love ;
'Tis the food the gods design thee,
Never at their gifts repine thee.
And for counsel which I owe thee
Merits high reward I'll show thee :
Glorious fate for thee in store,—
Just as poets prov'd of yore :

Bounteous meed I mean to shew thee ;—
Great good may the prospect do thee!
Thou and I—and all the same
Who inherit hopes of flame,
Trace them back to Noah's time—
Every age, and every clime
Prove the impress of that law
Whence our heritage we draw ;
Every poet since the flood
Sat, like thee, in maundering mood,
Pondering—-plaguing much, his brains
What could so ill reward his pains,
Wondering what the cause could be
That linked him to adversity :
Fooled, and foiled in every aim ;
Robb'd of life to purchase fame.
Well thou knowest the adage old,—
Mean't for beastly consolation,
Worthy being framed in gold—
Some quaint wits good lucubration :
Coachman, groom, or ploughman hind,—
What his station never mind,
Since sympathy and moral sense
Are not the fruits of high pretence :—
And wisdom saw true work to scan
Is—" Mark the maxim, not the man."
He was no dunse, wherever born,
Who said, " live horse and you'll get corn!"
Quote the proverb—note it down !
Trust me, brother, 'tis a true one ;
But, if stale thou deem'st it grown,
From it let us frame a new one ;
Let go the horse! he's but a brute,
And thou wilt stand his substitute ;
Public right in thee unaltered
Holds thee to its service haltered,
Toiling, thinking for the throng,

All the golden thoughts of song,
Check bit by oppression's rein
Yoked to penury and pain!
Caprice, whim, and folly's drudge,
*Not of thine own wants a judge!*
Malice, scorn, and crested spleen
'Gainst thy peace must all convene;
Earthly status, wealth, or favor,
Thou obtain them ;—never! never!
Hop'st thou good ?—chameleon's food
Dainty slops of thinest air!
Are the poet's surest food :—
Just think how nice thou'lt chew thy cud!
Gall'd by many a bitter feeling,
Barbed, beyond a Bard's revealing!
Whatever else thy soul may crave
Is garner'd t' other side the grave ;
Whence our adage let us frame,
" Die, poor Bard, and thou'lt get fame !"
    Would'st thou quell with rigorous scorn
Every base and vicious passion ;
    Would'st thou show where lurks the thorn
In the vernal flowers of fashion ?
Would'st thou probe corruption's vein,
Show mankind vice's stain,
Expose pride's every knavish wile,
Or rend aside the mask of guile,
Dash from its aim keen rancour's dart,
And show the leper in the heart ;
Tear off the sanctimonious guise,
The clack that hides from mortal eyes
The hypocritic arts, and plots
Of pander priests, and courtly sots ;
Peer thro' each loop-hole of deceit,
Forewarn the dupe, and paint the cheat ;
Expect not—that for this thy pains
Thou'lt need a clerk to count thy gains!

That gratitude on tiptoe, loud
Will twang her trumpet to the crowd,
And *crown with bays, and laud, and praise thee,*
An' high, to honour's summit raise thee,
That richest wines, and viands rare,
Will henceforth be thy daily fare!
That high and low will all regard thee,
And love and luxury reward thee!
Reverse the picture—mark thyself
Forsook by friend, and *minus* pelf!
Blotch'd envy, with her wry phizz'd throng
In fulsome slander lairs thy song,
The gaping crowd, with eager ear
Devours the clamorous rancid jeer!
Whil'st on thy heart, thou'lt bear the gash
Of many a coxcomb-critic's lash;
Wreathless thy brow, save lines which care
And painful thoughts have furrow'd there!
Thy honors, base detraction's mark,
Basely inflicted in the dark!
Thy board bespread with morsels stale
Of *blood-tax'd bread, and moon-struck ale.*
Whil'st love and luxury, may be
Such wits as leer and scoff at thee,
Yet, relinquish not thy aim:
" Poet die! and thou'lt have fame!"
Tho' thy life it cost to win it,
*Sure thy ghost may fatten on it!*
But if thou can'st, with mean grimace,
Chaunt servile odes to fools in place,
And basely, suppliant bow thy head
And ply the menial pander's trade;
Fawningly cour to self-poised knave,
Like hungry dog, or mindless slave!
Crouching with low debasing zeal
To kiss the rude unsparing heel
Which wanton cruelty or ire

Hath raised to tread thee in the mire!
Perchance—a Laureate's wreath may twine
Its degradation to the *nine!*
"Hence! spaniel thought, abhorr'd and vile!
"Thou meanest in a world of guile!
"Base nursling of the soulless breast
"By virtue's sunlight never blest!
"Can truth—can intellectual worth,
"The moral majesty of earth;
"Can Genius with the radiant eye
"Lit by the hand of Deity!
"Can aught to Bard or nature dear
"So far degrade thee from thy sphere?
"As thus, to don the weeds of shame,
"Whine for a crust, and barter fame?
Discard the thought, nor yield to shrink,
Whil'st thou art fit to toil and think;
Pursue thro' life thy nobler toil,
With conscience free from innate broil,
Light, if thou can'st with virtue's rays,
The erring heart that blindly strays;
Teach selfish iron-crested pride
How *Homer lived*—how Herod died!
Tho' sage and fool, may fail to prize thee,
Tho' knave and bigot both despise thee;
Tho' calumny and mean distrust
Should grind thy merits in the dust;
Still, foe to faction, schism and plot,
Bear every genuine poet's lot:—
Since each the others much resembles,
Despise the cringing wretch who trembles.
And, while Pegasus owns a wing,
And while Apollo reigns thy King,
Be Homer's lot and thine the same;
Poet die! and thou'lt have fame!

## ODE TO SPRING.

THOU art coming, gentle spring,
With thy zephyrs soft and sweet ; .
Through the wood, and o'er the mountain,
Whispering pleasure everywhere :
Thou art coming, gentle spring,
Now to garnish each retreat,
By shady glade and fountain,
With thy wreaths and pearlings rare :
Clothed in dews and light thou'rt coming ;
I can trace thee everywhere.

Thou art coming, lovely spring,
With thy incense and thy light,
And the balmy inspirations
Which thy vernal presence yields :
Thou art coming, cheerful spring,
With thy train of glorious bright,
And thy sacred scintillations
To the forests and the fields ;
And the song-birds hail thy coming
To the forests and the fields.

Thou art coming, happy spring,
With thy melody and mirth ;
All vocal is the wild wood
With thy welcome back again :
Thou art coming, happy spring,
With thy gladness back to earth ;
And the gems, and joys of childhood,
Richly sparkling in thy train :
How joyous rings the wild wood
With thy welcome back again.

Thou art near us, blissful spring,
With thy bounty-speaking smiles,

And thy hope-inspiring radiance,
Fresh from nature's fountain drawn :
Thou art near us, blissful spring ;
Hark ! the peasant, as he toils,
Joins the universal cadence,
As he tills the fertile lawn :
How he swells the rapturous cadence,
As he tills the teeming lawn.

Thou art with us, heavenly spring,
Full of promise, full of love ;
Ever bright'ning, ever blessing,
Is the progress of thy reign :
Thou art with us, heavenly spring,
From the angel-realms above,
With thy rays of glory chasing
Each fell shade of doubt and pain,—
Thou type of life immortal,
That shall burst from death again.

## EARLY GENIUS.

### AN ODE.

SEE ! where roams yon gentle child
    Beside the rippling stream,
Disporting 'mongst the blossoms wild,
    That on its margin gleam :
How dear to him those sunny hours,
    Unmarr'd by sorrow's shade ;
Life's pathways all seem spent with flowers,—
    Bright gems that ne'er can fade :
How rapt he views, with glistening eyes,
    The lustre of their bloom,

Their various forms, their varied dyes,
  And wooes their fresh perfume :
Time's young halo round his heart,
  Its blissful radiance doth impart,
Beauty, meekness, scent, and sound,
  Wreathe their fairy spells around ;
Ever warming, ever charming,
  Ever brighter seem the hours,
Around him, o'er him, all before him,
  Earth seems robed in fairy bowers !

Now behold him, wandering still
  Thro' the wild wood's shadowy glade,
Where, with emulating thrill,
  Nature's songsters charm the shade :
He feels—how like a sylvan king,
  The grove his regal hall ;
His throne is by the rock-born spring ;
  His courtiers minstrels all :
Unknown to him the wiles of art,
  Or fashion's tinsell'd show,
'Tis nature's morning fills his heart
  With pure and primal glow ;
As up his roaming vision turns,
  A latent spark within him burns,—
A thought—a throbbing sentiment—
  A wish—though now in durance pent—
That yet in living words shall breathe,
  And yield that brow a deathless wreath,—
Ever bright'ning, ever heightening,
  Kindling ardours proud and young,—
Trembling—gushing—upward rushing,
  Seeking numbers from his tongue !

Now yon mountain-track he keeps,
  Bounding 'mongst the heather-bells ;
Clambering o'er the rocky steeps,
  Where the echoes tune their knells :

More dazzling scenes, but still as pure
　From vice's base alloy,
To loftier march doth now allure
　The fond, romantic boy :
Proudly he bends his straining sight
　Where Alpine glories reign,
And panting with sublime delight,
　He leaves the tranquil plain :
See ! how boldly up he climbs,
　Where the dashing torrent chimes,
Where, with wild impetuous din,
　Loud it sounds o'er ledge and lynn,
Ever ringing, ever singing,
　Quaint responses to his glee,
As he chants the lay of his upward way,
　In a heaven-taught minstrelsy !

How rapturous ! pure in breath and brain,
　Wakes the weird light of fancy's morn ;　　.
Before the galling barb of pain
　The vision-web of life hath torn ;
While hope-buds, yet in embryo fold,
　Their rankling thorns conceal ;
And the sanguine heart deems all is gold,
　Which glittering hues reveal :
The hallow'd springtide joy of mind,
　Unmarr'd by venal pain,
Like-the incense of a summer wind
　O'er a fertile, flowery plain,
Buoyant through his heart is rushing,—
　All his fears in transport hushing,
And its glowing tribute fraught
　With the germs of noblest thought,
Ever spreading, ever shedding,
　To the broad, big noon of Time,
A heaven-born light, that may own no night,
　Till its latest bell shall chime.

There's a feeling in his breast,
  Ever young, and ever growing ;
A sacred passion, unexpressed,
  In proud and tameless ardour glowing :
Deep it beats, and high it swells,
  And it never more may rest,
Though 'gainst it every fate rebels,
  While a life-pulse stirs his breast :
'Tis ambition's wakening fire,
  Flaming higher, ever higher,
Ever burning, ever yearning,
  With unquenchable desire :
Nor penury, nor pain,
  Nor detraction's demon breath,
May quell that flame again,
  Till beyond the pale of death,
On the scroll of endless fame,
  Be inscribed another name.

## ODE TO A SNOWDROP.

HAIL, pretty little wildling gem !
  First offering of the year ;
Pure as the hoarfrost around thy stem,
  Thy silken folds appear.
Thy grassy home in greenwood glen,
  Beside the brawling stream,
Uncultured by the hands of men,
  Scarce greets the solar beam.

Fain would I sing thy graceful life,
  Like love, in humble guise,
In scenes obscure—mid hardship rife,
  'Neath frowning wintry skies ;

Not wintry fate—detractions bane,
  Nor penury's blighting sway,
Nor scorn, neglect, nor barbed pain
  The vital germ can stay.

Each little bird, whose cowering wing,
  Chill winter's langour bound,
Cheered by the promised glow of Spring,
  A welcome perch hath found ;
And ere the tardy frozen snow
  Has left the budding spray,
Seems to forget his carping woe,
  And trills a jocund lay.

Meek, lovely nursling of the snow !
  Deep in thy mossy bed,—
What power propitious, there below,
  Thy tender being fed ?
Thou claim'st no tithe of Orient hues,
  Or mellower sun-bow dyes ;
No nectar draught from April dews,
  No warmth from April skies !

First born of beauty !—thro' the wild,
  I love to trace thy bell ;
Emblem of virtue, reconciled
  In humble sphere to dwell !
Deep graven on the human heart,
  Should be thy sinless dower ;
Hope's blessings wake where'er thou art,
  Fair, modest, prophet flower !

## DIRGE OF THE MARINER'S WIDOW.

HE left me at morn on the shore,
  His bark was afloat on the stream,

And graceful, and gallant and grand
    She glided away like a gleam !
I stood on the shore, till his sail
    Sank far o'er the billows so blue ;
And I joyed in the favouring gale
    Tho' it wafted him far from my view.    .

A sigh, which I could not suppress,
    I heaved, as I turned from the shore ;
And a prayer for the loved one's success
    To the heavenly watchers it bore,
With slow and meandering pace
    I turned to the village again,
But oft-times my steps would retrace
    To cast a long look on the main !

I sank me that night to repose,
    And in vision recall'd him again ;
For I dream'd that a tempest arose
    And wrecked his fair bark on the main.
The lightnings were hissing around,
    The thunder's hoarse tumult was near ;
And piercing, and frantic, the sound
    Of his death-cry was dash'd on my ear.

Presentiment,—scoff not its power ;
    Existence is more than a dream,
There are bale clouds, that over us low'r,
    Revealed in the omen of dreams !
I groaned, and I pray'd and I wept ;
    And my anguish was bitter and long,
But whether I wakened or slept
    The peace of my spirit was gone !

Dark bodings its solace denies
    As daily I ponder in pain ;
And nightly ghast phantoms arise
    Midst the chaos that sickens my brain.

I sleep—but my slumbers are toil,
  I wake—but my fancies are dread ;
Stern misery makes peace to recoil ;
  And hope, the fair syren, hath fled.

Tho' oft with devotion I turn
  To the soothings of friendship and love,
In the desert alone I would mourn
  Like the hapless reft mate of the dove.
I hear the light laugh of the gay,
  And its rapture is hateful to me :
Oh, I wish I were with him, away
  In the measureless depths of the sea.

## THE STREAM THAT TURNS THE MILL.

INSCRIBED TO T. HAWKINS, ESQ., PORT ALBERT, BY
WM. BANNATYNE.

O' A' tha waters in the warld,
  Let ithers chant at will,
Gie me the haly humble stream
  That turns the gristin' mill :
Frae prince to peasant, wha but owns
  His heart with pleasure thrill
Wi' the merry music o' the brook
  That turns the gristing mill ?

Tho' nature's, seeming partial, hand
  Ne'er busk'd its brink wi' flow'rs ,
Ne'er crown'd its banks wi' sylvan shades,
  Cool grots nor fairy bow'rs ;
Tho' Beauty there wi' gaudy dower
  Ne'er deign'd to show her skill,
Yet, wha but lo'es the merry stream
  That turns the gristin' mill ?

Fu' mony strains o' venal praise
　　To ither streams are sung,
Since wild romance, on waverin' wing,
　　Her spells hath roun' them flung !
Or, commerce, wi' its thousand keels
　　Floats there, at wealth's proud will—
Forgetfu' o' the lowly stream
　　That turns the gristin' mill.

Nae classic grandeur marks its course ;
　　Nae towers o' lordly pride ;
Nae sculptured arches span its breast ;
　　Nae galleys stem its tide !
But bickerin' down some silent holm,
　　It wends—a nameless rill :
Whilst, fraught wi' blessings to mankind,
　　It turns the gristin' mill.

Oh ! mony a weary pilgrim wight
　　On penury's barren way,
It cheers wi' hope's inspiring glow,
　　By the magic of its lay.
And mony a portly, pamper'd wame
　　Wad own but sairlie fill,
If 'twerena for the thrifty stream
　　That turns the gristin' mill.

The simple gifts o' Providence,
　　Ah ! why should men despise—
Why scorn its meek realities,
　　And phantom treasures prize ?
Or, why should bards on unkent streams
　　Exhaust their tunefu' skill,
And pass, unsung, the canty brook
　　That turns the gristin' mill ?

O ! leeze me wi' the couthie clack
　　O' yon big plashin' wheel !

For dear I prize the dinsome gear
    That grinds our crowdie meal.
May gratitude for nature's gifts
    Our bosoms ever fill.
And aye we'll bless the merry stream
    That turns the gristin' mill.

## A PEASANT MINSTREL'S PLEA.

To toil for classic lore is vain
    To clothe a poet's tongue ;
Where slept the pedant's flossy strain,
    When blind old Homer sung?
'Tis not for bookworms measured phrase
    The glowing rapture sprung,
That graced the grand heroic lays
    Which Celtic Ossian sung.

The harp that loudest rings on earth,
    And sweetest sounds by far,
Was strung by one of *peasant* birth
    'Neath penury's frigid star!
It soothes the lovers teasing dream ;
    It lulls despair's alarm ;
It wakens mirth—it lights Hope's beam,
    And nerves the warrior's arm.

What mortal artist's tutored hand
    Could mould the flow'rets fair
That spring spontaneous o'er the land,
    Afar from culture's care?
What master's nice euphonic skill,
    Inspires the raptures loud,
That fire the lark's ecstatic thrill,
    Above the morning cloud?

D

The ornate tropes of verbal phrase
   May charm the puerile sphere,
Where flatt'ry strums its lukewarm lays
   In fashion's toy-toned ear :
As vocal chords shook by the wind
   No sentiment impart,
They own no heritage of mind—
   No melody of heart !

Oh ! tame had been the minstrel's fire
   And cold the human heart,
If none had tuned the vocal lyre
   Without the lore of art :
Not by scholastic rule is given :
   The soul's harmonious zest :
True eloquence is born of Heaven,
   And nursed at Nature's breast.

What marvel then if Nature's glow
   A peasant's breast should warm ;
And the rapt gifts of song bestow
   To music's loftiest charm ?
What marvel, if his rustic art
   Life's noblest flames should fan,
And teach, *still more*, the human heart
   " *The dignity of man ?* "

Let me enjoy the wide free range
   Of mountain, grove and dell ;
Where rural beauty girds the grange,
   And love and merit dwell :
The cataract dashing o'er the steep !
   The wierd old echoing caves,
The sylvan glens, and valleys deep,
   Where scented foliage waves.

The warriors' mounds—the martyrs' cairns,
   The fane's dismantled walls,

The stately ruins, grey and stern,
　Of ancient feudal halls;
To rhyme their various legends o'er,
　Amidst their ivy shades;
And tell, how crumbling pride, of yore,
　Our modern pride upbraids!

For since I was a tiny child
　I loved, in musing mood,
To roam the rough and pathless wild,
　And thread the mazy wood;
To ramble o'er the verdant plain,
　And on the shingly shore,
To gaze upon the heaving main
　And hear its billows roar!

To climb at morn the dizzy scaur
　When mists the vale did fill,
And watch the golden solar car
　Wheel up the eastern hill!
Or, when the twilight's changing hues
　Their fitful gambols play'd,
To sit and court the rustic muse
　In broom or hazel glade.

In summer's calm—in winter's storms,
　By land or foaming sea;
Oh! nature, all thy wild free forms
　Are beautiful to me!
Thine is the reign of lofty thought :—
　The pure Castalian spring,
Whence flows the soul inspiring draught
　Which tunes thy bards to sing!

I envy not nor much esteem
　The pampered hireling's bays,
Who strums his soulless Idyl theme
　In sycophantic phrase;

The servile task my soul would tire :
   Ev'n midst th' applauding throng,
I could not wake a Laureate's lyre
   And lack a freeman's song.

But give me life's congenial charms .
   The proudest boons I prize ;
The hearts which social virtue warms
   With gen'rous sympathies :
Th' souls whose bright celestial beams
   No despot's frown can tame ;
I ask, on earth, no loftier themes
   To sing my way to fame.

## A PSALM OF FUTURE LIFE.

THERE 's a happy country far away beyond the
   waves of Time,
Beyond the flight of sun and stars—a pure and
   cloudless clime ;
Its fields of never fading bloom are always warm
   and fair,
And no corrupt or noxious weed e'er shows its
   presence there.

Its fountains are of clearest sheen by earthly slime
   untinged,
In lambent glory rippling on, with deathless verdure fringed,
Thro' bowery beauty's chastest scenes forever on
   they stream,
Secure from Winter's gelid breath, the Summer's
   scorching beam.

Its groves are all of spicy trees with fruits of stary ray,
That glisten with inviting smiles from every scented
    spray ;
The feather'd songsters 'midst their boughs are
    nesting free from dread,
For no marauding raven there its wings shall ever
    spread.

Its pathways lead thro' fragrant vales by fresh'ning
    zephyrs fann'd,
O'er flow'ry meads extending far, and mountain
    prospects grand ;
No dangerous pitfalls hidden there—no craggy
    stone to wound,
Nor snake to bite the pilgrims' heel, in ambush
    there is found.

On every summit's azure height there stands a
    beauteous shrine,
With dome of brighter gold than e'er was dug from
    earthly mine ;
Where anthems of celestial love, and songs of
    grateful joy,
In rapturous peans ring, from tongues unstained by
    earth's alloy.

'Tis always spring in that pure clime—'tis always
    noontide fair,
No tempest ire can blight its bloom—no night
    cloud gather there ;
Its dwellers' duties, all are praise, no racking toils
    they prove,             [bounded love !
Their high reward the precious meed of God's un-

Eternal youth illumes each face—each brow is
    smooth and fair,
No furrow'd cheek—no age dimm'd eye—no time-
    scathed form is there ;

The fount of health and vigorous spring wells up
    in every heart,
And pours its salutary tides thro' every vital part.

No dwelling rear'd by mortal hand need they
    wherein to rest,
Nor care nor cold which mortals feel shall e'er their
    homes infest ;
No galling stripe from tyrants' rod—nor hunger,
    pain nor fear,
Nor semblance of the slightest woe which mortals
    suffer here.

No spirit clogg'd by Mammon's rust—no conscience
    scar'd by sin,
No heart array'd in traitor's guise shall access have
    therein ;
No base seducer's syren wile—nor dark detractor's
    lore
Shall triumph o'er a victim's heart or probe its
    bleedings more.

No self-debasing pander wretch who gloats a
    despot's will,
And plies the satrap's masked blade a brother's
    blood to spill ;
Who heaps his burden on the weak, or mocks the
    stricken mind,        [grind.
Nor he who lifts his iron heel the lowly poor to

Who never shields from misery's storm the helpless
    outcast's head,
Who robs the widow of her mite—the orphan of
    its bread ;
Who fattens on his neighbour's wreck or hoards the
    spoils of crime—        [clime.
Shall never have inheritance in yonder sinless

The soul relieved by penitence from Error's vicious
    sway,
By earnest vigils back restored to Virtue's sacred
    way ;
Or they whom sublunary lust hath never yet de-
    filed—
The faithful priests of Nature's law, the patriot and
    the child.

The salt of earth, the meek, the true, the generous
    and the wise,
Who never swerve from duty's call whatever lures
    entice ;
Such only, in yon realms of bliss, shall shout tri-
    umphantly,
" Where is thy sting, O Death, and where, O Grave,
    thy victory ? "

Come spirit sick of earth's dark ways, its poignant
    cares and toils,
Its passions—venoms, that beset like adders from
    their coils !
Lay down thy martyr'd fleshly load with unreluctant
    faith,
And praise Thee for yon happy realm beyond the
    gates of death.

There kindred spirits on the shore, all jubilant shall
    throng,
To hail another child of light, with joyous shout
    and song ;
Their forms in stainless vesture clothed, of radiant
    tissue wove,
The chosen and redeem'd of God, and fostered on
    his love ?

## THE CITY OF THE DEAD.

THERE is a city, down yon vale,
Where balmy fragrance scents the gale,
Where first the dewy crocus springs,
And first the homely redbreast sings,
Where first the pearly tints of morn
Fall twinkling on the flowery thorn,
And the wild rose, with simplest grace,
Folds in the bower-tree's close embrace ;
Where, 'neath the yew's umbrageous gloom,
The daisy, meek,—and primrose bloom ;
And where the thrifty spider weaves
Its web among the burdock leaves ;
Where first the bee his rapture tells
Within the honeyed foxglove bells ;
Where sweet at noontide sings the wren,
As, safe within her briery den,
She views with pride her tender brood,
Secure from hawk, or magpie rude ;
Whilst to the brook that murmurs by
Faint echoes yield a quaint reply ;
And sweetly pensive breathes the gale
O'er yonder city in the vale.

Who are the citizens, whose homes
Comprise those rows of grassy domes ?
Who, whilst without the vital world
In passion's vortex vast is whirl'd ;
Whilst commerce, science, art, and creed
The ire of rival factions feed ;
Whilst rapine, riot, lust, and crime
Deface the chronicles of time ;
Who, whilst in jubilation loud,
Exultant shouts the giddy crowd,
In hero-homage, round the car
That bears the demigod of war ;

Unmoved by all the mad acclaim,
Heed not the blatant trump of fame ;
And all unconscious of the blast,
See not the pageant hurrying past ;
Who, whilst in sorrow's wild alarm
O'er vanquished Freedom's mangled form,
When her brave banner, soiled and riven,
No more can woo the breeze of heaven,
And trampled midst a nation's gore,
Can lead the patriot forth no more ;
Whilst rending moan and frantic pray'r
Swell the dire tumult of despair,
Till nature, in her caves below,
Reverberates with excess of woe ;
All unmoved, respond no wail,
In that city down the vale !

" What are they ? "   Inquirer know,
In that city, still and low,
Stand memorials old and new ;
Some are false and some are true ;
Graven there, on stone or brass ;
Note each record as you pass :
Each brief legend will repeat
" There the past and future meet :"
What the *past ?* it boots not now ;
They, perchance, have been as thou :
What the *future ?* none may say,
Till the final judgment day :
Note the *present*, as we tread
Round that city of the dead :
How still ! oh, how serenely still !
No ring of anvil, clack of mill ;
No strain of pipe or harp they hear,
No clarion-crow of chanticleer,
No din of trade's tumultuous crowd,
No thrill of war's fell clangour loud,

No jar of wealth's proud chariot wheel,
No hissing storm, no thunder peal,
No shriek, no groan, no yell of strife,
No sound that shakes the halls of life,
No voice of dissonance or wail
Disturbs that city in the vale !

No selfish want, no wild desire,
No scowl of ruthless tyrant's ire,
No festering wound by malice given,
No sigh from hearts by treachery riven,
No galling probe of mental pain,
No grief that battens on the brain,
Nor penury's accursed form,
Nor fell remorse's canker-worm,
Nor vile seducer's dastard art,
Can there profane the human heart :
Vain fashion's fluctuating whim,
The wretched miser's sordid dream,
The lecher's lust, the coward's fear,
The coxcomb's vaunt, the scoffer's sneer,
The slanderer's dart, the grin of hate,
The blight of scorn, the gossip's prate,
The hapless maniac's frenzied gaze,
The mad blasphemer's reckless phrase,
The conscience-smitten murderer's stare,
The haggard aspect of despair,
Gaunt superstition's goblin train
Can never haunt their homes again ;
Free from mortal fear and ail,
In that city down the vale !

Let howling storms the forest tear,
And bellowing thunders rend the air,
Let prone magnetic billows roll,
And shake the earth from pole to pole,
Let rude ambition's impious aim
Life's holiest altars wrap in flame,

Let fierce contending factions rage,
And wreck the world from age to age ;
In that city down the vale
Throbs no pulse of mortal bale :
Done life's conflict, toil, and dread ;
Each within his silent bed,
Lull'd in nature's dreamless rest,
Wrongs, nor cares, nor fears molest :
Oh, how tranquil ! how sublime !
O'er them glides the stream of time !
Where, with passion's banner furl'd,
And at truce with all the world,
In the womb of mother earth,
Calmly they wait their second birth !

## MY LAST WILL.

WHEN life's teasing dream is o'er,
Every busy pulse at rest,
And its cares and pains no more
Can affect my brain or breast ;
When my heart, in silence deep,
Freezes in its chilly sleep,
And my rigid form lies hid
'Neath the darksome coffin lid,
Every throb of joy or sorrow
Ne'er to greet a fresh to-morrow,
Bear me to some tranquil glen,
Where, beneath the twining bushes,
Far remote from selfish men,
Some pure, nameless streamlet gushes ;
Where the robin, merle, and wren
Chant their happy, simple songs,
Grateful that each shelt'ring den
Proves a shield from craven wrongs ;

Where the modest, little flowers,
Twinkling in their mossy bowers,
Tinged with nature's chastest hues,
Freshened by her purest dews,
Strown to bless the wilds of earth,
Claim from spring the earliest birth ;
Far from fortune's cultured care,
Types of worth in humble sphere ;
Where no yew nor cypress' gloom,
Shading sculptured marble tomb,
Tells where titled dust lies pent,
'Neath its storied monument :
Where the slanderer may not come,
Where the scoffer's voice is dumb,
Where detraction's cloven tongue,
Though to syren sweetness strung,
May not charge one sacred cell
Where the holy echoes dwell :
Dig me there my lonely grave,
Lay me down with honest care,
'Tis the only rite I crave :
" Carve me no mementos there ;
Pile the mould, and smooth the sod ;
Sigh, and leave the rest with God :
Back in mother nature's breast,
Oh, how soundly I shall rest ! "

## A DYING HUSBAND'S ADDRESS TO
## HIS WIFE.

O JEANIE, spread my pillow doon,
    And tie my aching brow ;
I've meikle need o' kindly han's
    To lift and lay me now ;

I've meikle need my weary e'en
  To steek in peacefu' rest :
O place thy a'e han' on my back,
  The ither on my breast.

Fu mony a lang and dreary scene
  O' life I've journeyed thro' ;
And mony a daurg o' painfu toil
  My brain's been doom'd to do ;
But licht to me ilk burthen seem'd,
  Whilst health and strength I kept,
And poortith's cauld unhallow'd scowl
  Ne'er owre our hallan swept.

And, Jeanie, tho' misfortune's ban
  Hung owre our lowly bield,
And haggard want, wi sunken e'e,
  Its gaistly form revealed ;
I never heard your murmuring word,
  But aye your cheerfu smile,
Fra mirkiest broodings o' despair
  My spirit back could while.

I've strave against the waes o' fate
  In many a shaded hour ;
Tho' lang, alas ! the rankling thorn
  Lay pent within the flower ;
And simple tho' my nature seem'd,
  And humble tho' my claim,
I scorn'd to be a tyrant's tool,
  Or earn the bread o' shame.

Now lay me down, my gentle Jean,
  And press my throbbin brain ;
And place a'e saft han on my heart,
  That aft has sooth'd its pain ;
But dinna sab, nor wauk the bairns ;
  I've kissed them whaur they sleep,

And ca'd the angels doon fra heiv'n,
   Kind watch owre them to keep.

I couldna bide to see them greet,
   Owre soon the warst they'll ken,
The struggle o' this cauld rude warl,
   And craft o' selfish men ;
The snares o' vice that hidden lie
   On a' the paths o' life ;
The cankering wounds o' hopes deferred,
   And passions fell and rife.

And you maun strive, when I am deid,
   And teach our wee anes a'
To trust in providence divine,
   And act by honour's law ;
The bite that's stown, however sweet,
   Turns bitter in the end ;
A conscience pure is aye at least
   The soul's most faithfu friend.

You maunna fret, you maunna pine,
   Nor wail when I am gane ;
You'll dootless hae a heavy care,
   And want's a weary train ;
But stievly stan' wi honest thrift,
   And let the bairnies ken
To lean on earth's cauld charity
   Is no the gate to fen.

- Now fare thee weel, my gentle Jean,
   " You aye were kin' and true ;"
And tho' I lang to be at rest,
   I'm laith to part wi' you !
You'll come gin spring to yon kirkyard,
   Whar dark-leav'd boortrees wave,
And bring the bairns, wi sweet wee flow'rs,
   To busk their father's grave.

## STANZAS,

Suggested by the calamitous circumstance connected with
the death of Capt. James Thorburn, by drowning
in Lake Huron, June 5th, 1868.

'Twas morn—and June in sunny pride
O'er Huron's far expanded tide,
It's richest smiles diffusing wide
    Poured with unwonted radiancy.
No sullen cloud's portentous form
With omen-scowl presaged the storm ;
And stretch'd in slumbering beauty's charm
    The mighty lake heaved gracefully.

Then homeward bound across the flood,
With full spread sails—the breeze that wooed—
A little bark her course pursued,
    Slow-gliding, trim and steadily.
Each heart on board with hope beat high—
No seething vortex eddied nigh :—
No treacherous reef nor shoal was by
    To mar their full security.

The wish'd for haven seemed so near—
Its glittering spires, its roofs and pier
Reflected, on the waters clear,
    A scene of magic brilliancy.
The master and his little band
With pride surveyed the prospect bland :
Tow'r, wood, and stream, and winding strand
    Far blent, in bright serenity.

There rose the shrines affection reared,
To parent, child, or spouse endeared,
Where beckoning love, and worth revered
    With smiles stood welcoming.

And long before the evening's ray
Would leave the sky to twilight grey,
Fond joys should all their toils repay
    Midst scenes of kindred unity.

But fleet as from the cannon's womb
Bursts forth the bellowing thunder's boom,
And furious as the mad simoon
    Raves in its wild velocity !
So darting from his aerial cell
With livid glare, and frantic yell
Careering on his mission fell,
    The tempest fiend shrieks direfully !

Now shade on shade, in deepening fray,
Fast shrouds the day-star's struggling ray ;
And shook by dread magnetic sway,
    Down rolls the lurid canopy.
Around the babbling billows crowd ;
And hoarse, from forth the rifted cloud,
The prone tornado, ravening loud,
    Sweeps with terrific vehemency !

High swells the tumult's nearer sway,
As upward wheels the hissing spray—
Not mortal art could now pourtray
    That scene's horific majesty !
Each fear-smote sailor shrinks aghast !
Some grasp the shrouds, some clasp the mast !
One breath of pray'r,—and landward cast
    One gaze of 'wildering vacancy !

The thousand ties that bind to life,
The sireless child, the widowed wife !
Come crowding mid the harrowing strife
    To swell the hearts dread agony !

'Tis come !—the fatal stroke is given,
In lashing fury ever driven,
With masts submerg'd and keel to heaven,
        Midst smothering foam she's weltering.

No life boat comes, no friendly sail,
Here pause, for nature drops her veil,
Let fancy glean the sad detail
        Where reft hearts wail their misery.
Whose cry rings o'er the mirky wave ?
Who calls for help where none can save ?
Who toils with strong-nerved arm to brave
        The overwhelming surge of destiny ?

Who, like the corsair king of old,
Drench'd by the billows, numbed with cold,
On upset prow maintains his hold
        With unrelaxed tenacity ?
Who, with wierd hopes inspiring zeal,
Whilst clinging to the slippery keel,
Prone through the plank with blade of steel
        His life's last hold scoops dexterously.

Who sternly toils—but toils in vain
'Gainst gaunt despair and mental pain,
'Till every pulse in breast and brain
        Subsides in death's rigidity ?
Thou Thorburn !—brave, sincere and kind ;
Of manly heart and noble mind,
Whose worth in many memories shrined
        Shall live thro' long futurity.

From infancy to manhood's prime,
With ties that strengthened still with time,
I've watch'd thy course, with pride sublime ;
        And gloried in its purity.

E

Thy heart in virtue's vigour bold
Was framed in nature's amplest mould
In friendship, truth, and worth untold
   , It glow'd with meek benignity.

Deep mouldring in thy watery tomb,
No earth flowers o'er thy breast may bloom ;
But friendship long shall mourn thy doom,
   And love-lips lisp thy memory.
And high above in joyous light,
Where earth's rude storms can bear no blight ;
Beyond the shades of death's drear night
   Thy soul has soared triumphantly.

---

## ELEGY

### FOR THE LATE THOMAS M'QUEEN.

#### I.

'Tis sober eve—the sun's last lingering gleam
In Huron's farthest placid wave doth hide,
And paler stars, with cool and pensive beam,
Look languid, glimmering o'er the silent tide.

#### II.

The summer strains that late in greenwood fold
Burst in rapt notes to charm the ear of day ;
Hush'd—like some tale in Syren numbers told—
Resign to sadness each lorn vacant spray.

#### III.

The murmuring Maitland, slowly gliding near
The dark green foliage, dirge-like sighing round ;
Blend their sad tones in Fancy's dreaming ear,
Deep fraught with many a quaint familiar sound.

### IV.

Hail, genial twilight—Nature's holiest hour!
Bard, Priest, and Sage thy soothing influence own ;
Day's gaudy tumult still'd : Reflection's power
Resumes it's sway, and reason claims her throne.

### V.

Beneath those branching boughs whose deepening
    shade
Looms o'er yon calm sepulchral scene,
I mark the mound beneath whose sod is laid
The Sage, the Patriot, and the Bard McQueen.

### VI.

He sleeps with Death, that cold and ruthless power,
Whose mighty fiat lays earth's loftiest low,
Mourn Canada! thy friend in evil hour
Lies crush'd in dust by Fate's unerring blow.

### VII.

Soundly he sleeps life's well-fought battle o'er,
Nature's brave son, whose soul's unwavering flame
Might claim the heroes meed—in whose heart's core
Was shrined the Truth, that purest pearl of fame.

### VIII.

Gone to the Grave! the wise, the good, the great,
The manly purpose, and the feeling heart ;
All levelled by the direful stroke of Fate,
Wail Canada! not thine a common smart.

### IX.

The great souled ministrel, full of human love,
Whose ardent effort, whose untiring zeal
'Gainst Malice, Scorn, and base Corruption strove
Whose aim was still the Universal weal.

### X.

Not midst the gay and giddy ranks of pride,
Where ostentatious servile minions bend,
Kept he his vigils, watching favor's tide;
His homage stoop'd where man could man befriend.

### XI.

Oppress'd humanity, where'er it groan'd—
In dungeon cell, or wandering in exile—
Alike his sympathetic ardor owned,
His genius sooth'd—his counsel taught to smile.

### XII.

Not his the flimsy gloss of flippant lore,
The tinsell'd tones of proud scholastic art;
But warmly gushing from his bosom's core
In native phrase he pour'd his noble heart.

### XIII.

From Ostentation as from Falsehood free,
'Gainst despot might thro' life be bravely strove;
With glowing eloquence in every plea,
Exalting Mercy, Friendship, Truth and Love.

### XIV.

Fair Love, (whose raptures o'er his early lyre
Wreath'd the fond spell of many a soul-born strain,)
Which nought of Fate on earth could bid expire,
Nor time, nor toil, vicissitude nor pain.

### XV.

Despite the lights and shades which chequer'd time
Had strewn profusely o'er life's devious way,
His Fancy oft retraced that far, fair clime,
The mountain home of Life and Love's young day.

### XVI.

To trace again the round of early years,
Their social bonds, true hearts, and friendly ties,
Where, mingling in the shade of youth's compeers,
He shared their pastimes, aims and sympathies.

### XVII.

Alas! down Retrospection's vista, prone
There rolls a river on whose voiceless shore,
The wreck of many a daring hope lies strewn,
To light life's strife again—ah! nevermore.

### XVIII.

Vain with its current, toils the panting soul;
Proud Fame her beacon light displays in vain;
Resistless onward to that dismal gaol
Of Shades Plutonian rolls its tide amain?

### XIX.

The sweetest treasures of the human heart;
Mind's loftiest visions; Art's unfathom'd lore;
In quick succession on its breast depart
To swell the gloom of Lethe's dreamless shore.

### XX.

Thus, crowding on his mind's reflective gaze,
Hope dash'd on hope; adown the eddying wave,
Swept the dense pageant of life's vanished days,
The proud, the humble, to a nameless grave.

### XXI.

And thus he sighed :—"Oh Change! thy mandate
    stern
Can all ambition's towering schemes subdue?
Let Genius here the awful lesson learn,
It's futile toil earth's bubble Fame to woo!"

### XXII.

" Hence, dark absorbing vision !—dust to dust—
I too, must follow in my turn ! " he cried ;
" Beyond the tomb—lo ! Mind's immortal trust
Dispels earth's dreary pangs," he said and died.

### XXIII.

Mourn Canada—with unfeigned sorrow mourn ;
The truly noble and lost deplore !
Gone to the Grave—forever from thee torn ;
Soundly he rests, life's bloodless battle o'er.

## EPITAPH.

THOU who in contemplative mood may'st stray
Within the precincts of this solemn scene ;
Mark well this mound, and read this little lay,
'Twill teach what he beneath in life hath been.

If Patriotic worth thou can'st admire ;
If Native Genius thou dost revere ;
If in thy soul thou lov'st the heaven-strung lyre,
The grateful homage of thy soul pay here.

If at the beck of impious mortal power,
Thou ne'er was't known to bend the servile knee,
If thou at Mammon's shrine could never cower,
In suppliant, sordid, mean idolatry ;

If brooding over woe's unshielded lot,
Thou pliest the helpful mite, the feeling tear :
With sympathetic fervor bless the spot,
A kindred heart, a Poet's dust lies here.

If thou art selfish, vain and insincere,
A mean idolater of power and pride,
Mock not his memory with one feigned tear,
Thy mask resign, and learn of him who died.

## STANZAS.

### ON THE DEATH OF A FAVOURITE CHILD.

HARP o' my heart, thy jarring strings
   May wauk nae strain o' joy;
The plaintive murmurings o' my grief
   Maun a' their notes employ;
A waukrife sorrow racks my breast,
   Aud scathes my throbbin' brain;
And a gloom upo' my spirit hangs
   Like a nightmare's broodin' pain.

There's a wee grave down yon dowie dell,
   Where, sound in death's still sleep
Lies ane—our dearest treasured bairn,
   In the silence dark and deep.
There, rigid, pent in pulseless fauld,
   That sinless heart maun byde,
That throbbed, as 'twere but yesterday,
   Wi' life's exultant tide.

We hear nae mair her siliery voice,
   That kindly saft and clear
Its tickling tones o' happiness
   Shed, warbling on the ear;
We see nae mair thae flaxen locks
   That graced her bonnie bree,
Nor the glowin' beams o' sunny life
   That sparkled in her e'e.

Thae dimpled cheeks—thae rosy lips,
   Wi' love smiles mantling o'er,
Now blanch'd in dark corroding blight
   Lie hid forever more.
And daily—nightly—ear' and late
   My restless spirit sighs,
And hovering haunts the dowie dell
   Whar our wee Katie lies.

'Tis sad to prove that holiest hopes
   Are earliest dashed wi' gloom ;
That sweetest flow'r-gems first maun droop
   And shed their vital bloom ;
And ah ! how sad, that childhood's life,
   Affection's fondest tie,
Maun bear sae aft, the direful blight
   O' death's dread destiny !

Alack ! how vain is mortal pride !
   So fragile is its trust !
A silken chord just snaps in twain,
   And beauty turns to dust ;
So briefly passed, our fondly loved,
   To grim cauld death's embrace,
Wi' the life-light shimmering in the e'e,
   And the love-smile on her face.

Oh ! spirit o' our gentle bairn
   Frae mortal bondage free ;
Nae pang o' earthly anguish mair
   Can penetrate to thee !
But, while thy early loss we mourn
   To thee the boon is given,
To share a holier love than ours,
   Midst deathless light in heaven.

Oh ! speed away thou winter wild,
   That wreathes her tomb wi' snaw ;

And haste thee here, thou mild breath'd spring,
  That wooes the flow'rs to blaw ;
I'll plant sweet gowans on her breast,
  And the wild rose at her head ;
And the birds will sing soft lullabies
  O'er our wee Katie's bed.

## OCTOBER.

### A SKETCH.

Now surly, hoarse October's frown
  O'er flood and forest scowls ;
The waves are torn to hissing spray,
  And drear the woodland howls.
With biting breath the icy cloud
  In boreal rancour lowers,
To sicken nature's halcyon bloom
  And scathe her vernal bowers.

Oh ! where is now the rural charm
  That hallow'd hill and plain,
Whilst love and beauty filled each hour
  And danced to hope's sweet strain ?
When shepherds piped by sunny brooks,
  And wild birds gaily sang,
And blythe, from fields of golden corn,
  The reaper's carol rang.

The hoar-frost, in its crispy robe,
  Hath sheathed the dewy green ;
The daisy folds its starry eye,
  And droops its head unseen.
In fitful murmurs down the brake,
  The leafless willows sigh,

And pensive echoes now respond
    A dirge-like melody.

The lark beyond the rainbow's rim
    Hath hush'd his rapturous lyre,
And peacefully 'mid scenes obscure
    Evades the raven's ire.
The swallow on her flight hath sped,
    In quest of milder skies ;
And, ominous of winter's storms,
    The carping snow-bird plies.

The bee hath sought her honeyed hive,
    From rustic toil set free,
And, grateful of her life's reward,
    Hums o'er her social glee.
Whilst harpy broods with hungry rage
    Scream fiercely on the wind ;
And madly court the certain doom
    That waits the vicious mind.

'Tis thus with life—with human life—
    When fleets the golden prime ;
When beauty wastes, and passion cools,
    Beneath the blasts of time ;
When withering eild with icy touch
    Lowers like the boreal storm,
Congeals the fountains of the heart.
    And seres the shivering form.

When fell adversity's dire cloud,
    Surcharged with ruthless woes,
Looms deeper as the shortening day
    Approaches to its close.
When melody forsakes the ear
    And light forsakes the eye,
And toiled in pain and brooding gloom
    Writhes every vital tie.

Love, friendship, joy, and wealth, and power,
　Ambition's motley train—
How futile then the dream sublime
　They nurtured in the brain !
" Who would not prize a calmer faith
　To sooth his spirit's care,
And bear him o'er the woes of age
　Unshaken by despair ?"

# DIDACTIC AND GENERAL SENTIMENT.

## ACROSTIC.

HUMANITY hath read thy horrid tale,
   And turns disgusted from the slander-
     ous page,
   Rudely, but vain thou rend'st the se-
     pulchre,
Raking the relics of the noble dead,
In hopes to prop a baseless infamy.
Enduring, as the tenure of his fame
To whom the title of a bard is due,
Time hath embalm'd his memory to the world,
Even those who in the rivalry of life
Bestrew'd with jealous spite, his wayward
    path,
Embitter'd his best hopes: and scoff'd his
    muse ;
Envied his fame, and toiled to cast contempt,
Cruel, and wanton, on his early lays,
Humbly, humanely, honourably mute,
End at his tomb the records of their spleen.
Robe thee in weeds of moral purity,
Suffuse thine eye with tears of saintly love,
Take virtue's throne by semi-pious storm,
One British poet, forty years interr'd,
Will oftimes visit thee, and on thy heart
Engrave the hateful name " Calumniator."

# A TRIBUTE TO THE MEMORY OF THE
# ETTRICK SHEPHERD.

THE July sun was hot and bright,
  The marshy pools were dry ;
The startling heifer madly pranced,
  Stung by the venom'd fly.
The fiery tide of summer's heat
  Flow'd in its noontide pow'r,
Its scathing ire the verdure crisp'd,
  And blanch'd the meadow flow'r.

Beneath a hedge-row high and green,
  Pent in the cooling shade,
Upon a soft and grassy couch,
  A shepherd's boy was laid ;
In slumber's sweet refreshing fold,
  His eyes were gently closed,
And at his feet his faithful dog,
  Half-consciously, reposed.

The lucid vision-scenes of youth,
  · In fair perspective train,
To rapturous measures stirr'd by song,
  Held revel in his brain ;
And Fancy's gay but sinless forms,
  In light and beauty moved,
And Hope, and Truth, and Honour's smiles
  Ennobled all he loved.

In panoramic train afar,
  Along the welkin blue,
Life's loveliest, and its wildest scenes,
  Burst glowing on his view ;

On many an unsung hero's brow
    He traced the crown of fame :
Bequeath'd for deeds of nobler worth
    Than history sought to name.

In many a rural dingle deep,
    And dernly-shaded glen,
He traced the holiest shrines of love,
    Unknown to " courtly ken."
In groves, and dells, and streams unnamed,
    He saw, with minstrel pride,
The gorgeous maze of life's romance,
    In beauty's prestige dyed.

How long he slept—how long he dreamed—
    It boots me not to sing :
Suffice—the radiant hours flew o'er
    On swift seraphic wing ;
But, o'er his heart and o'er his brain,
    A spirit now held sway,
To rule the future of his life,
    And gild or cloud his way.

To him each morn the matin song
    Burst sweeter from the sky,
And all the landscape glories round
    Shone fairer in his eye.
With prouder step he climbed the fell,
    And view'd with prouder gaze
His country's mountains blue and free ;—
    Bright streams and flowery braes.

And oft he tuned his rebec small,
    And strove to sing by turns
The hallow'd patriot tunes of old—
    The glowing strains of Burns.

The deeds of Scotia's martial sires,
　Her oral legends wild,
With ardent fancies thrill'd the mind
　Of this lone mountain child.

The intercourse of books and men :
　The powers by science sway'd,
Had never sought his rustic home,
　His mental toils to aid.
To him the tutor'd phrase of schools,
　Their symbols ev'n unknown,
On Nature's breast to manhood rear'd,
　He grew as Nature's own.

The roaming maniac's fitful dirge
　His plastic fancy fired ;
The wandering ballad-singer's lay
　He conn'd with zeal untired ;
To hear the sturdy beggar's tale,
　Thro' tedious hours he'd wait :
The vagrant chapman's phamphlet lore
　He long'd to emulate.

Thus Genius thro' his youthful mind
　Its strong inflection wrought,
Till learning's fount at length unsealed
　For him its pleasing draught ;
Then, prone as breaks the murky cloud
　When orient sunbeams throng,
So brake the spell that wrapt his lyre,
　And woke the shepherd's song.

Throughout fair Scotia's wide domain,
　And many a distant clime,
Wherever genius claims a shrine
　Of homage link'd to time :

Worth's sacred honours gild his name,
    And deathless fame's reward
Hath crown'd that humble dreaming boy :
    The Ettrick Shepherd Bard.

---

## SONG.

I HAD a bonnie dream yestereen,
    O' hame and happy days ;
Enrich'd wi' many a glorious scene
    'Mang Caledonian braes.
The haunts o' boyoood's sunny time,
    Frae cloudy care sae free,
In native grandeur blest again
    My memory's dreaming e'e.

Ilk furrow'd fiel, and braken knowe ;
    Ilk valley, ben, and cairn ;
Ilk gowan bank, and craigie brow
    O' aspect bauld and stern ;
Ilk roving brook's meandering path,
    The gladsome shaws amang ;
Ilk woodlan' screen o' shadowy fauld,
    That wooed the cushat's sang.

It seemed to me the summer's prime,
    When fresh frae every fell,
Awoke the fragrance o' the thyme,
    And hinnied heather bell ;
The roving bee's untiring hum,
    Ilk flow'ry pathway fill'd,
And high in air its lofty lay
    The rapturous lavrock trilled.

F

The Fox-glove's purple pendles hung
    Adown the mossy glades,
And sweet the meek wee blue bells sprung
    Amang the broomy shades ;
Whilst prouder o' their statelier bloom
    The haw and slaethorn vied,
And the rowan wi' its tassell'd croon
    Adorned the mountain side.

The shepherd piped on cliffy steep,
    Where freedom's echoes rang ;
And frae the lochs blue bosom deep,
    Loud rose the boatman's sang ;
And many a loved companion's voice,
    And favourite burnie's croon,
Cam mingling on my throbbing ear,
    Wi' soul-entrancing soun'.

I felt myself again a boy,
    In life's unclouded morn,
And sighed to hug ilk wild free joy,
    That laucht a' care to scorn ;
I twined wi' flowers and rashes green,
    A garland for my head,
And deem'd the withering touch o' time
    Wad never bid it fade.

The merry rair o' rural fun
    I joined wi' loud giffaw,
And stark wi' glee the game to win,
    I kicked the big foot ba'.
I shared anew ilk weel-kent play
    Upon the old schule green,
And chased wi' glee the *baukie bird*,
    Aroun' the stacks at e'en.

And syne, when closed the gloamin's e'e,
    I sought the hamestead hearth,

And clamb wi' pride my father's knee,
   My happiest seat on earth ;
He lugg'd me to his honest heart,
   And blest me o'er and o'er,
And taught me virtues maxims leal,
   As in the nichts of yore.

'Tis sweet to dream o' childhood's hours,
   And soul-stored memories :
O' distant, long-forsaken bowers,
   And a' their hallowed ties ;
But ah, 'tis sad to wake again
   In regions far awa,
Wi' freezing eild coiled roun' the heart,
   'Mang storms o' drifting snaw.

## THE GOWAN IN AMERICA.

### AIR—" *The Old Oaken Bucket.*"

My wee modest gowan, sae crimson and pearly,
   Kind mentor o' youth and its gowden hours gay,
Frae the green sunny fields o' thy kindred I ferlie
   What mandate has will'd thou should'st wander
      away?
Why com'st thou to pine in the land o' the exile,
   Sae uncouth and dreary and far frae thy hame ;
Nae biel to defend thee, nae kind hand to tend
   thee,
   Unprized for thy virtues, unkent by thy name?
My wee modest gowan, my lowly sweet gowan,
   Why roam'st thou a stranger sae far frae thy
      hame?

Saft fell the spring on thy meek tiny blossom
   To nourish thy stem and to freshen thy hue :

And pure were the zephyrs that fann'd thy young
    bosom
  Sae starlike at morn wi' the sunlicht and dew.
The lark, frae her nest in the greensward beside
    thee,
  Soar'd high in her rapture to chaunt in thy
    praise,
And fond lovers roamin' through love-haunts at
    gloamin',
  Aft hung on their pace on thy beauty to gaze;
My wee pearly gowan, my crimson-tipt gowan,
  Thou'rt far frae the love-haunts o' life's early
    days.

Here 'mang the dark forest shadows sae eeri,
  Whar chill hoary winter lags dowie and lang,
Whar stern scowlin' fate, wi' an aspect uncheery,
  Forbids e'en the birdies to wauken their sang;
Ah! whar wilt thou fauld thee, thou lame simple
    stranger,
  I sigh when I think o' the weird thou may'st
    dree,
Sae lowly, sae tender; alas! for the danger,
  Fair nursling o' Nature, attending on thee?
My wee tender gowan, my pure modest gowan,
  Thy presence gies pain, fraught wi' pleasure to
    me.

Thou speak'st o' the meads, where to childhood's
    gay measures
  Wi' licht pace I've danced on the green dewy
    swaird,
O' hope dreams lang flown, and a thousand soul
    treasures,
  Lang pent in the gloom o' the silent kirkyard.
But come, simple mentor o' scenes lang departed,
  Nor deem I could lea' thee neglected to pine,

Frae scaith I'll defend thee, wi' kind hand I'll
    tend thee,
Lane flowret, thy fate is an emblem o' mine.
My meek lowly gowan, my wee pearly gowan,
    Thou'lt hallow my bower wi' the dreams o'
    langsyne.

## THE WEE BALLAD SINGER'S COMPLAINT.

RESPECTFULLY INSCRIBED TO M. GIBSON, ESQ.

I'M a wee orphan laddie, and Tammy's my name,
And on earth I hae neither got kindred nor hame ;
I'm forced to sing ballads to earn my bit bread,
Tho' oft while I'm singing I wish I were dead.
There's something forbids me to beg or to thieve,
Tho' there's plenty wad wile me to baith I believe ;
Some talk o' a workhouse ; I wadna gang there,
Tho' I'm a puir bairnie and naebody's care.

My father was dead lang before I was born,
And my mother was left a puir widow forlorn ;
They tell me she never had ony but me,
And she ca'd me her hope and the licht o' her e'e;
She knitted and washed, and she span and she
    darn'd,
And aye our wee morsel in honesty earned ;
And she sang to me whiles, tho' her heart it was
    sair,
And as lang as she leev't I was somebody's care.

But my mother she dee't, and they burie't her deep
Mang the cauld gloomy pits whar the died bodies
    sleep ;

And they cover'd her owre wi' the clay and the
    scraw,
And her biel and her blessin' for aye seems awa ;
How wildly I grat when they hid her frae me !
Ere the saxth hapless winter o' life I did see ;
How I sabb'd a' that nicht owre her eerisome lair !
A lanely wee bairnie and naebody's care.

There's nane that sae aften I meet ony airt,
As the feelin'-less folk wi' the cauld staney heart ;
There's nane in whase presence I coor wi' sic
    pain—
" Ah surely they canna hae bairns o' their ain ?"
For I ken by the stern callous frown o' their e'e,
They neither hae awmous, nor kindness for me,
And a glamour aft clouds me, amaist like despair ;
I'm a puir bairn, and naebody's care.

Sometimes in my sleep I've a vision fu' dear,
But 'tis aye when I'm hungriest its sure to appear !
'Tis a man and a woman that bend owre my bed,
And baith claisp their hans owre my wee dreamin'
    head !                                    [speak,
They mutter some words, and they smile as they
And syne kneel beside me, and kiss ilk a cheek !
And their words seem to sound like my kin' mither's
    pray'r :                                [care !"
" That heiven aye micht mak' her lane bairnie its

Oh ! I wish I were deid—or, I wish I were big,
And awa frae the toons, on the waves, or the rig,
Wi' the strength in my arms aye befittin' my toil,
Whare'er I micht fen' on the sea, or the soil ;
I think I'd get clear o' the scorn and the pain ;
And I ne'er wad come back to sing ballads again ;
The ane or the ither maun aye be the pray'r
O' the lanely puir bairn that is naebody's care.

'Tis no' on the selfish, the vain, or the mean
That the shelterless hearts o' the hapless may lean,
Ae kin' glowin' smile frae a guid body's e'e
Is worth a' the scauldin's the paughty can gie ;
O ! leeze me wi' folk that's guid natur'd, tho' poor ;
And shield the wee wand'rers that sing at their
    door :
May wintry misfortune ne'er fa' to their share :—
Its a puir bairn that is naebody's care.

## TO A SKYLARK.

HAPPY Skylark ! tow'ring singer !
   Rapturous herald of the day !
Morning's stars delight to linger
   On their paths to greet thy lay.
From thy bed among the daisies,
   Fluttering high on dewy wing ;
Just as Dawn its curtain raises,
   'Tis thy joy to soar and sing.

Up, where man holds no dominion,
   Where his vision fails to pry,
Hailing morn on twinkling pinion,
   Vocal spirit of the sky !
On thy track the shepherd ponders,
   As thou wend'st thy heavenward flight,
Loves thy lay—but deeply wonders
   What inspires thy loud delight.

Thrush and Robin, Merle and Linnet,
   Lilt from bow'r, or greenwood spray ;
Their's the carol of a minute,
   Thine the music of a day.

Up ! amidst the golden daylight,
　High o'er valley, wood and hill,
Making from grey dawn till twilight
　Cloud and rock and forest thrill.

Swains may pipe when echoing valleys
　Far the winding notes convey :
Harps resound in festal palace
　Where resort the proud and gay ;
Dulcet voice and skilful fingers
　Wake but tones of fitful flame ;
Thou art nature's noblest singer,
　All their strains to thine are tame.

Far from earthly song companions,
　Where no ravening hawks pursue,
Boldly thy seraphic pinions
　Dip in heaven's ethereal blue.
Fervid noon more bliss instals thee,
　Loftier, louder wakes thy thrill :
And, when eve to earth recalls thee,
　Down thou flutterest singing still.

Tell me—happy skylark ! wilt thou ?
　Whence the measure of thy mirth ;
Tho' a home on earth thou'st build thee,
　Are thy passions not of earth ?
Man, the dupe of fraud and folly,
　Carps of care and tyrant wrong ;
Thine the mission sweet and holy,
　Blending earth and heaven with song.

Would that I could sing but near thee !
　Would, thy happiness were mine !
Would some cherub wings might bear me
　To that pure free realm of thine !

Partners there in sweet vocation,
  Free from earth's discordant crowd,
We would join in jubilation,
  Brother minstrels of the cloud.

---

## SONG.

OW'RE the green meadow, and down by the brook
  Eagerly tracing the promise o' spring ;
Tentily prying in every neuk,
  Wistfu' I wander and pensively sing :
Come forth, ye treasures o' youth's bonnie gowan-
    lea !
Come forth, ye tassels o' hawthorn and rowan-tree!
Come a' ye charms that, in youth on my glowin' e'e,
  Shed purer wealth, than the pearls o' a king.

Wauken—thou lavrock, thy lay on the cloud !
  Rich was thy heavenly rapture at morn :
Lift thou sweet lintie thy melody loud ;
  Harp, thou green craik, mang the saft-braided
    corn :
Goudspink, and canty wren, down in the brierie
    shaw,
Break ye the spell o' the dark winter's eerie law :
Thou blythsome mavis—to hail the spring's cheerie
    ca'
  Pipe frae thy spray, on the cream-blossom'd thorn.

Whar's the wee crawflow'r that bloom'd on the
    brae ?
  Whar's the meek harebell, that blink't mang the
    fern ?
Whar's the wee primrose and goukbell sae blae ?
  Whar's the red foxglove, that wav'd on the cairn ?

Whar are they a', that in youth sae delighted me,
And out wi' the sang birds o' mornin' invited me ?
Sair tho' the warld, and its rude cares hae blighted
    me,
    Still, for their sakes I could yet be a bairn.


Whar's the lown glen, wi' its saft mossy knowes?
    Whar's the wee burnie that bicker'd between ?
Whar's the wee lassie that plighted her vows
    Aften to me, in the broom-shades at e'en ?
Whar now's the sweet-scented slaethorn, that
    flourish'd there ?
Whar a' the friendships and loves that I cherish'd
    there ?
Whar a' my glowin' heart foster'd and nourished
    there :
    Wilt thou—oh, springtide! revive them again ?


Thus, as I wandered by forest and mead,
    While Nature mak's vernal the breast o' the year ;
Life's early memories inwardly plead,
    Joys long departed again to appear ;
Langsome I gaze—as I fancy that youth, again
Ought to restore a' its beauty and truth again !
Shout in the spring a' its glad notes to soothe again
    Hearts which adversity canna mak' sere.


## ELEGY TO MY AULD COAT.

My auld brown coat, my ain brown coat !
    Thou ance wert fiel and braw ;
'Tho' now thread-bare and ablins mair,
    Thou'rt rax't by mony a flaw,

Yet, laith I'd be to part wi' thee,
   That aft hast beek't life's flame,
When frost and snaw in frigid ca'
   Assail'd my shiverin' frame.

I bought thy claith and trimmin's baith
   In Sandy Frazer's shop ;
Just twa pun ten thou cost me then—
   Nay tawdry snobbish slop ;
But weel waive tweed to suit my need,
   And paid for, richt aff han—
I neir took pride to cleid my hide
   Upo' the credit plan.

Wi' shears and tape, thy douce trim shape,
   My freen McCrindle clipp'd ;
And sew'd ilk part wi' dexter art,
   Sae strang it never ripp'd.
I paid his bill wi' ready will :—
   " Nae tick," quo' I, " for me ; "
Now ten lang years midst joys and fears
   We've borne gude companie.

Since thou'st been mine in days langsyne,
   Fu' mony a gate I've been ;
And mony a blast has o'er us past .
   O' rigour snell and keen ;
But, bien and warm, and free frae harm,
   Weel button'd up in thee,
Thy guid braid claith frae wintry skaith
   Has aye protected me.

Some coats I've seen o' gaudier sheen
   On backs whar nane should be—
Backs that should catch the deepest scratch
   A nine-tailed cat could gie.
I've kent some, too, and ken them noo,
   Conferring warl's respect

On trickster's slee wha ought to be
   In tar and feathers deck't.

There's mony a coat o' broider'd note,
   O' crimson and o' blue,
Wi' epaulette o' rank beset,
   And star-gemm'd breist on't too.
In court's carest, wi' lofty zest
   The wearer acts his part ;
And yet within that tinsell'd skin
   There beats a coward's heart !

Some coats o' black could tell a crack,
   Had they the gift o' speech :
How thochts an' deeds ignore some creeds
   Despite what priests may preach.
It's no a' gloom, like raven's plume,
   A spirit pure may show :
The lark chants loud abune the cloud,
   The raven croaks below.

My auld brown coat ! my faithfu' coat !
   Before I put thee aff,
Earth shall behauld, proud in thy fauld,
   A Poet's photograph !
Should dandies geck—their disrespeck
   Will ne'er gar me complain ;
An honest pride's a noble pride—
   Thank heaven, thou art my ain.

We've baith grown auld, and friens look cauld
   That fawn'd in better days—
Oh ! mean, mean Earth ! where human worth
   Is valued by its claes !
Full mony a chiel, whose merits leal
   A hero's meed might claim,
Maun starve unknown, whilst round a throne
   Is nursed a Nation's shame !

Weel lined, and strang, thou'st stood the bang
    O' mony a ragin' blast ;
But like myself, time 'gins to tell
    Thy tug o' strength is past.
Wi' patch and sleek full mony an eke
    Thy use till now sustain'd,
But wind and weet, and blirtie sleet
    Nae mair thou can'st defend.

O' woolly nap, a hamespun hap,
    I now maun seek the charm,
Thir wintry days need thicker clathes
    To keep an auld man warm.
'Tis Nature's plea that thou by me
    Should'st be in eild proteckit,
And no like slave a tyrant knave
    Thrawn oot to de negleckit.

Thy frail auld age I will engage
    Shall ne'er insulted be
By mean abuse—nae vulgar use
    Shall e'er be made o' thee.
Thou'lt ne'er be ta'en by han' profane
    To scour nor pot nor pan ;
Nor yet be cuist mang mangy waste,
    In Ralph the ragman's van.

This cleek o' beech, beyond the reach
    O' mouse and ratton baith,
Shall bear thee up, wi' kindly grup
    Bune meuseless vermin scaith ;
And then thou'lt hang, auld freen', as lang
    As I hae breath to draw,
Tho' rogues should sneer, and coxcombs jeer,
    An honour to my wa'.

Whilst to my mind some memories kind
    Aft times thou will restore ;

Nae ghaistly dun I've cause to shun
    Whate'er may haunt my door ;
But fringe or rag, whilst there you wag—
    Whate'er vain gowks assert—
There's nane daur say but, in thy day,
    Thou'st happ'd an honest heart.

## POVERTY SECTION.

### A. L. S'S REPORT.

Up in the bush in a certain direction,
Lies a School district call'd Poverty section :
Poverty stricken in all sorts of senses ;
Beggar'd in intellect, wreck'd with expenses,
Pester'd by prejudice, spleen, and confusion,
Plung'd in a vortex of mental delusion :
Grumbling and grovelling in every direction :
Discord runs rampart o'er Poverty Section.

'Twas a subject of strife from its very formation,
Begging, and prigging, and fierce litigation :
Meetings in public, and meetings in private,
Always uncertain what point to arrive at,
Meeting each distance from outline to centre,
Choosing a site was a clam'rous adventure ;
Next came the size and the mode of erection,
Bones of contention for Poverty Section.

Next in the matter of choosing a Teacher,
Some would have Dominie coupled with Preacher,
Some for a dear one, but more for a cheap one,
Whilst some  thought it far too expensive to keep
    one :

Threatening Trustees with condign immolation ;
Haunted to death by the ghost of taxation :
'Twas a fruitless endeavour to make a selection !
Befitting all notions in Poverty Section.

'Tis rare to attend all their annual meetings,
And their note how blatantly cordial their greetings !
How fawningly courteous, and lovingly civil,
In tones of fraternal affection they revel ;
What grasping and squeezing of hands ! most
    untiring,
For each others welfare, like brothers enquiring ;
You would deem that the pure soul of zealous
    affection,
Inspir'd every bosom in Poverty Section.

But truce mark the change when the chairman is
    chosen,
How tongues all turn forked and wag by the
    dozen !
How every ones fang in his neighbour's heart
    tingles,
'Till the house quakes with caption from basement
    to shingles :
'Twould be vain to recount all their whimsical
    topics—
Suffice it no scene 'twixt the Poles and the Tropics,
Could ever produce such a motley collection,
As oft is discussed up in Poverty Section.

Tug at the purse-strings of chronic economy,
Talk about libraries, globes or astronomy ;
Mention such subjects and try how they'd relish
    them ;
Pencil and pen both would fail to embellish them.
*They* sell their wheat, or their oats, or potatoes,
For such childish toys as a school apparatus ;

They would think you were seized with lunati
    infection,
A dangerous member in Poverty Section.

Oft the chief theme of their virulent squabble,
And one about which they incessantly gabble ;
At home and abroad with unspairing avidity,
Showing the strength of native stupidity,
Showing the seeds of condign animosity,
Poisoning the ear of humane generosity :
Is maligning the Teacher in every direction,
Prone to expel him from Poverty Section ?

Foiling his temper with brazen audacity ;
Sneering and chiding his lack of capacity ;
Mulishly callous his morals degrading ;
All his expressions and actions upraiding :
If he has virtues, they've filth to fling over them,
If he has talents, they cannot discover them !
Were he the archtype of humane perfection,
He'll find persecutors in Poverty Section.

Every thing placed to retard and to puzzle him ;
Some would cajole him, and others would muzzle him!
Some prone to backbite and others to bully him ;
Were he as pure as a cherub they'd sully him :
If there is one who would sweeten his chalice,
They mark him the target for cannon mouth'd
    malice ;
Treat him as tainted with rabid infection :
A furious bugbear in Poverty Section.

Some have a notion that truly is comical,
Extremely ludicrous, but still economical :
'Tis that a child who is kept out at labour,
Should learn quite as much as his school going
    neighbour ;

If to the school roll his name be appended,
That ought to serve tho' he ne'er should attend it;
Should he prove doltish, the whole imperfection,
Is charged on the teacher, in Poverty Section.

Sometimes it happens—when selfish cupidity
Softens the pulse throbs of billious acidity:
Some craven scout with a fawning servility,
Angles around with the bait of civility;
Praises the progress he makes with his scholars,
And urges in fine that he needs a few dollars,
Which if he lends him—next annual election
He'll pledge him his vote at, in Poverty Section.

Oft the Trustees too, with crawling docility,
Make themselves tools with a bogus gentility;
Pompously futile, or dozend by dotage,
They barter their power for a mouthful of potage:
Sway'd by self interest—or mental opacity;
They pander like Pilate to mobbish voracity:
Vainly to them need he sue for protection;
God help the teacher in Poverty Section.

Strange! a community, living as neighbours,
Helping each other in out of door labours,
Practicing friendship with earnest grimaces,
And rigidly tucked up in Piety's laces;
Flocking in compact to hear the same preachers;
Cannot agree about schools and their teachers:
One would suppose, upon gravest reflection,
They ne'er should have either in Poverty Section.

G

## A BARD'S GRATITUDE.

### TO THE POPULATION OF GODERICH.

ANCE mair in my couthie wee biggin' at hame,
Stay'd up by the smiles o' my bairnies and dame,
To my freens in the city in duty I sing,
O ! the gratefu' emotions within me that spring ;
For tho' the warm flush of excitement is past,
On my soul the impression is destined to last,
At least till the moment when death steeks my e'e,
For their kindness to "auld minnie Scotland" an' me.

 "Their kindly bit treat to my minnie and me,
 Their dainty bit treat to my minnie and me ;
 I trust that ungratefu' I never can be,
 For their friendly regard for my minnie and me."

Aye proud o' her bairns was my minnie, kind dame,
When worth brocht them credit abroad or at hame ;
But she aye had sae mony that claim'd sic respect,
That the fost'ring o' ane caused the ithers neglect ;
She had sodgers and sailors and sage lads in law,
And skilfu' machanics, musicians and a',
And Bards—I repeat it wi' tears in my e'e—
To whom she seem'd step-minnie mair than to me.

 " Tho' whiles scarce a biel had my minnie for me,
 Whilk caused me fu' many mishanters to dree ;
 Nae stain on her honor I'd e'er wish to lea',"
 And I ken she'll be proud o' your kindness to me.

Lang time hae' I harp'd till my pow has grown hoar,
O' her grandeur, her glories, her virtues and lore :
How the stalwart invader she humbled langsyne,
For my creed seem'd the love o' that minnie o' mine !
And still tho' far distant I won frae her shore ;
Tho' fated to tread on her green-sward no more,

I ken her auld heartstrings 'll tingle wi' glee,
When she hears the respect ye paid her in me.

> " Your kindly respect for my minnie and me,
> Your halesome respect for my minnie and mo ;
> That a Bard sae much priz'd in his lifetime
>     should be,
> May justly gie pride to my minnie and me."

Fu' little I ween'd as I thrumm'd on my lyre,
And fann'd the faint glead o' the auld Doric Ire,
That ever in scenes so remote there should reign,
A heart-pulse responding the thrill o' my ain !
That bosom's congenial were throbbing sae nigh,
To the dirge o' my sadness or lilt o' my joy,
Whase kindly affection should urge them to gie ;
Sae wauly a heeze to my minnie and me,

> " Sae wauley a heeze to my minnie and me !
> Sae timely a heeze to my minnie and me !
> That auld senseless maxim o' ' *Wait till ye dee,*'
> Ye've cancell'd at last for my minnie and me."

Now lang may your echoes by greenwood and brae,
Respond to prosperity's jubilant lay !
May each hall and each cot, every hamlet and grove,
Be the temple of virtue, contentment and love !
May wealth smile on industry—worth walk in light—
Intelligence, beauty and freedom unite !
Enshrin'd to your honor, the honor ye gie
To auld farrant freends like my minnie and me.

> To auld farrant freens like my minnie and me ;
> The honors ye've gi'en to my minnie and me ;
> Ye may trow sic's my pray'r till the moment I dee,
> For your haly respect to my minnie and me.

## WINTRY SENTIMENTS.

### AN ODE.

HEIGH-HO ! this wintry weather !
  How each bitter storm :
Wind, and snow, and frost, together
  All life's bowery haunts deform !
All the hopes the spring-day nourish'd,
All the joys that summer cherish'd ;
All the fruits of autumn perish'd ;
Oh ! how bleak the sky of life is !
Oh ! how stern this innate strife is !
Thus I sigh, and this I say :
Heigh-ho ! and alack-a-day !
How soon youth's visions fade away !

Once for me, on earth, were beaming
  Love and friendship's light ;
And affection's ardent dreaming
  Poised my spirit's soarings bright, .
Life was social, sweet and jolly ;
Free from pain and melancholy ;
Never dreaming trust was folly !
Oh ! how pure was life's full chalice ;
Unprofaned by woe or malice !
Thus I sigh, and this I say :
Heigh-ho ! and alack-a-day !
How fast life's fondest ties decay !

No more for me, on earth is shining
  The light of love's bright eye ;
Toil, and grief and age combining,
  Cause me ever thus to sigh—
Heigh-ho ! but life looks dreary !
Wrapt in wintry clouds uncheerie !
Hopes deferred makes hearts so weary ;

And stem cold Truth dispel each vapour
That woke round Fancy's luring taper.
Thus I sigh, and this I say :
Heigh-ho ! and alack-a-day !
What sorrows haunt an old man's way?

No more for me on earth is calling
   Kind friendship's syren voice :
Frail age and penury appaling
   Ne'er were friendship's partial choice,
When the spells of age have caught us,
Friendship, that in sunshine sought us,
Fleets with all the gifts it brought us.
Selfishness sub-bornes its pinions :
Swiftest wing'd of Fortune's minions !
Thus I sigh, and this I say :
Heigh-ho ! and alack-a-day !
It leaves us when it ought to stay.

No more for me on earth are wreathing
   The flowery gift of praise ;
Time his searing blasts bequeathing
   From my brow hath reft the bays.
Traitor Fancy ! why deceive us?
All the chaplets thou dost weave us
Fade when youth and fortune leave us ;
Hapless eild and wintry weather
Prove thou'rt falsehood altogether.
Thus I sigh, and this I say :
Heigh-ho ! and alack-a-day !
Oh ! when when will misery pass away !

## SONG.

In the spring of our life, when our hearts are as free
As the heart of the lambkin that frisks on the lee,

Our path lies thro' sunshine, o'er moorland and plain;
And our bow'rs are the shades of the deep hazel glen.
We love the calm dell where the rath daisy springs,
An' the green leafy boughs where the glad robin sings;
We love the blythe tones of the brook's rippling din,
And we joy in the dash of the hoarse brawling lynn.

How lovely the hills in their purple array,
Tow'r upward to welcome the dawn of the day,
Or gleam in the light of the clear silv'ry moon
As they woo'd her bright smiles in the still nights
        of June !
How dearly each haunt and fair pathway of youth,
Seems hallow'd by nature with beauty and truth ;
Nor fame, love nor fortune can lure us to roam
Whilst our fondest affections are centred at home.

How rapt Fancy revels with credulous joy,
On friendships, and loves unprofaned by alloy ;
Or peers thro' the future, undaunted by dread,
All holy and fail as the landscape we tread ;
When all that we hear of the wiles and the woes,
And the ruin of hearts, that from treachery flows
We reckon as fables, our bliss to restrain,
Or phantoms that flit o'er insanity's brain.

But woe's me for time, and the changes it brings,
When the home-hearth is chill'd by the blight of its
        wings !
Alas ! for the anguish that sickens the heart,
When the tender and true, from love's circle depart;
When the pleasures we cherish'd are destined to die,
Like flow'rets that wither as noontide draws nigh ;
And hope, like a harp o'er which discord hath stole,
No joy-notes melodious can sing to the soul.

When far far remote from our infancy's clime,
Exposed to the conflicts and dangers of time ;

Like barks blown adrift on adversity's sea,
Despair for our pilot, and rocks on our lee !
When the pole-star is hid, and the watchers asleep,
And frantic with tempest the rude billows leap !
When the magnet is lost—thus, bereft, on life's main,
Oh ! who would not sigh for his childhood again ?

## SONG.

AIR—" AN AULD MAN CANNA DAUNTON ME."

FELL malice with her rancorous tongue
Assailed my heart when very young,—
With many a lure and ruthless blow
She sought to dash life's cup with woe ;
The earliest hopes whose radiant beams
Illumed my life's-spring's holiest dreams,
My fondest aims and efforts true,
She strove to daunton and subdue.

CHORUS—To daunton me ! and I so young,
   With dastard dart and syren tongue !
   But still with all its perfidy,
   She ne'er could fairly daunton me.

In youth when vigour's glowing tide
Did fresh in heart and brain preside,
With sturdy face and uphill strove,
My goal the sphere of peace and love—
Of peace and love untinged by shame,
And competence to guard the same,
Still envy with her cloven tongue
Essayed to daunton and to wrong.

CHORUS—To daunton me, but all her skill,
   Tho' prone to work my downfall still,
   Some inborn power sustained my plea,
   And aye she failed to daunton me.

In many a realm beneath the sky
I've sought my various destiny,
Midst many hopes and many cares,
Beset with wiles and unseen snares ;
With industry, and truth, and song,
In solitude and city's throng,
I've braved detraction's direst power,
And sing undaunted at this hour !

CHORUS—To daunton me ! tho' I am old,
　　　　However crafty, base, or bold,
　　　　Whate'er his pride or title be,
　　　　A false knave dares not daunton me !

But why, this maxim good and wise,
My infant mind was taught to prize ?
I learned it in my cradle song,
Fresh glowing from my mother's tongue,
That worth, and truth, and conscience clear,
Whatever course in life I'd steer,
Would guard me still by land or sea,
Whate'er might deign to daunton me.

CHORUS—To daunton me I need not tell
　　　　What wrongs thro' life to me befel ;
　　　　But still, despite all perfidy,
　　　　They ne'er could fairly daunton me.

## THE BONNIE WEE STAR.

THERE'S a bonnie wee star 'yont the path o' the mune,
'Tis the meekest and purest that sparkles abune :
Like the soft e'e o' love in the calm gloaming hour
It 'lumines my soul wi' its mild haly pow'r ;
It wooes me awa frae the turmoil and din
O' this strife-weary warld and its temples o' sin,
To pore on its peacefu' and mild gouden light,
Till far in its circuit it fades frae my sight.

I've foster'd my spirit, thro' lang years o' care,
Wi' glints o' a hame that awaited me there :
A hame free frae tyranny, poortithe and wae ;
Where nae wiley serpent daur lurk to betray,
Where nature a' sweet in its primitive bloom,
May ne'er bear the sunblight nor scathing simoom,
Whare sin canna enter ; and death canna mar
My Eden o' bliss, in yon bonnie wee star.

Away frae the warld, and the gloom o' its graves,
The ire o' its tyrants—the groans o' its slaves ;
Beyond where the eagle can soar in its flight :
The tract o' the whirlwind—the shroud o' the night,
Where toil never sickens, and love never fades ;
Where malice and selfishness never invades,
Where the soul ne'er pines o'er its hopes lang deferr'd,
And the wail o' reft friendship hath never been heard.

I've ca'd on the angels that wait on the leal,
And waft them frae wae to the regions o' weal,
To speed on their journey and bear me above
Thro' the blue haly lift to yon fair realm o' love ;
Ae truth hallow'd spirit awaits on me there,
Whom fell fate can rend frae my bosom nae mair
She smiles frae yon portals and beckons afar,
Inviting me hame to my bonnie wee star.

---

## OUT ON THE OCEAN.

OUT on the ocean—away from the land !
In our swift bounding bark, o'er the billows so
    grand !
Careering in tempest, how proudly we sweep !
O ! what so sublime as a life on the deep ?

Far out on the ocean, away on the main,
We race with the dolphin and porpoise again :
How tame are the pleasures of city or field,
To the soul-stirring joys which the ocean can yield !

Majestic our freedom ! unlorded our realm !
We course as we list by a stroke of the helm ;
So buoyantly borne o'er the foam-crested waves,
We dread not the storm-fiend tho' frantic he raves.
Each spar bending freely ! each sail widely spread !
We gallantly leap o'er the surges ahead !
Huzza ! how we rush o'er the billows so grand,
Far out on the ocean—away from the land !

Away from the land, with its cities and tow'rs !
Its toys, and its temples, its thrones, and its bow'rs!
Its tinsell'd delusions, its lusts, and its pride ;
And its altars, which gory ambition hath dyed !
From its turmoils, its vices, its guile, and its arts,
And its passions, that gloat on the ruin of hearts :
From its vortex of souls that commingle in crime,
O ! how pure is the ocean ! how free ! how sub-
      lime !

We once loved to roam on the green sunny earth ;
To cull its gay blossoms, and shout in its mirth ;
And still there's a ray of our destiny's star
That beacons our course to some haven afar.
We count on the rapture which time hath in store
When the friends of our hearts circle round us on
      shore ;
'Tis for these hallow'd feelings our vigils we keep,
Abroad on the ocean—away on the deep !

## THE BIRDIES AND ME.

I'VE aye had a feeling of britherly love,
For a' the wee birdies that lilt in the grove ;
Frae the wren in the fauld o' the laigh turnin' brier,
To the blackbird that sang frae the tree-tap sae clear;
So fitfully joyous on pinion or spray,
They mingled their notes a' the lang simmer day ;
And e'en when the gloamin star glanced o'er the lea,
'Twas hey dey and sang wi' the birdies and me.

How aft hae I wander'd in bright flowr'y June,
Awa fra the clamours and care o' the toon,
Mang the lown-bughted shades o' the green forest
    glade,
To mingle my strains wi' the carols they made !
Our wild varied anthems concerted we sang,
Till the sweet sylvan mazes wi' melody rang ;
I doomed life a simmer that never wad syne,
And I fancied their feelings were kindred to mine.

Their lives were like mine, and as free frae a dread,
O' the snare o' the fowler—the claw o' the gled :
Their loves and their freedom they chanted
    unmarr'd,
Those dearest o' birthrights to birdie and bard.
They sang tho' the simmer was waneing awa,
And leaves turnin' yellow wi' tints o' the fa' ;
Their blythe hearts like mine frae suspicion was free,
Nae bodings o' wae had the birdies and me.

The storm-clouds are raving amang the bleak hills;
And hoarse grows the music o' burnies and rills ;
The brown scatter'd leaves in each pathway are
    spread ;
And a hoar crispy cranreuch lies cauld on the mead!

For his rowth cozie byke the wee bee quits his moil,
To sip the rath hoard o' his lang simmer's toil ;
But whars the warm biel, and the soul cheerin' fare,
That the wee modest minstrels o' nature should
    share ?

Now gurly October, wi' ominous glow'r
Foreshadows the scathe o' the dark coming hour,
The woodlands are leafless, and murmurings drear,
Fa' fitfully sad on the pain-stricken ear !
Thus life wi' its visions o' brightness departs ;
So the ravage o' time chills the fires of our hearts ;
'Tis dool in the groves that sae late rang wi' glee,
For 'tis winter, alas ! wi' the birdies and me.

## SCOTIA'S FAMOUS ROBIN.

Young genius roamed by a bickering stream,
    In the lown o' a birken glen ;
And his fancy was wrapt in a rhyming dream,
    Unknown to selfish men ;
And he struck his free toned hamely lyre,
    And wakened the echoes roun',
Till it seemed as some rapturous rhyming choir
    Responsively hailed the soun'.

Nae vaunt had he o' great pedigree,
    Nor o' stie and courtly name ;
But his heart was sound and his mind was free,
    And his brag was a freeman's claim ;
And he struck the chords wi' as bauld a han'
    As minstrel e'er did draw ;
And sang in despite o' pride and might,
    That a man was a man for a'.

The minstrel was nae schule bred wight,
    Force fou' o' classic lear ;
But he read Auld Nature's book aright ;
    And he toiled for a rustic's fare :
And he sang wi' the birds in the leafy groves,
    O' his Mary or his Jean ;
And he warm'd his heart in the lowe o' love,
    In some rural bield at een.

O ! leeze me wi' the patriot flame,
    Saft fanned by music's breath !
For it bursts the bonds o' slavish shame,
    And it scorns at the dreid o' death ;
Its shrine is high in the mountain land,
    Which despot ne'er could awe ;
Where the guardian glaive o' the Wallace brave,
    Show'd a man was a man for a'.

Whare'er the gales o' Simmer roam,
    Or the storms o' Winter ring :—
Away on the ocean's crest o' foam,
    And whare'er the wild flow'rs spring ;
Where shepherds pipe on the sunny hills,
    Or the War-triumph rends the air :
The harp o' Coila blends its tune,
    And her Minstrel's name is there !

Then awa' wi' the boast o' lordly state,
    And its toy-toned warblings tame ;
'Tis the great in mind who are truly great,
    On the deathless scroll of Fame !
As the wood notes wild o' Nature's child,
    Tho' bred 'neath a roof of straw,
Hae link'd this claim to Robin's name,·
    That a man is a man for a'.

## A NURSERY RHYME, TO A NEW TUNE.

Come awa, my wee lassie !
Toddle owre to me, lassie !
Come to daddie's knee, lassie !
    Stumpin' a' thy lane !
Dinna be afraid to tumble !
Gie yer mammie back her thimble :
Here's a sweetie thou can crumble :—
    Pussie will get nane !

Haud your handies oot, lassie !
Stap wi' 'tither foot, lassie :—
Dinna keek about, lassie !
    Craw and cythe to me ;
Dinna thraw thy bonnie lippie !
Floorie isna very slippy :—
There my thoombies, take a grippie—
    Noo ! thou'st on my knee.

Here's yer sweetie noo, lassie !
Put it in thy mou', lassie !
Thou'st thy daddies doo, lassie,
    Aye sae blythe and fain ;
Thy wee face sae fair and glossy,
Nestlin' kindly in my bosie,
Wi' its glintin' smiles sae cosie,
    Lauch awa its pain.

Clap thy daddie's cheek, lassie—
Tho' thou canna speak, lassie,
Ilka merry freak, lassie,
    Tells me a' ye mean ;—
Tho' my face is *frau* and *fretty*,*

---

* Old Doric phrase for brown and withered.

Thae sweet looks—my bonnie pettie,
Tell me that ye think me prettie :—
    Blessin's on yer een !

Loup and frisk, my wee lassie,
Nane daur spoil yer glee, lassie,
Ilka fling ye gie, lassie,
    Makes me loe thee mair !
Caprin brisk to daddie's jingle,
Gars his heart wi' pleasure tingle ;
Thou was sent to bliss our ingle,
    My wee dawtie fair !

Mony a paughty loor, lassie,
Wha on dad looks doon, lassie—
Some that wear a croon, lassie,
    Half their wealth wad gie,
Just for ae wee tigmaleerie ;
Ae wee ruddy dainty dearie,
A' their ain—like thee sae cherrie,
    Dancin' on their knee.

## SONG OF THE AXE.

### AIR—"THE BRAVE OLD OAK."

A SONG for the axe ! the woodman's axe !
    With its edge so keen and bright !
For the proudest halls that grace our land
    Have been reared by the axe's might.
From the primal hut in the forest wild,
    To the modern regal tower,
From the rude canoe to the war-ship huge,
    All progress owns its power.
        A song for the axe, etc.

Then sing to the axe, the woodman's axe !
  That stretches the forest low,
That clears the tract for the ploughshare broad,
  And the sunbeam's fostering glow,
Till the graceful corn with the golden ear
  Waves over the fertile soil ;
And the garden blooms in the wilderness,
  Rewarding the woodman's toil !

      Then sing to the axe, etc.


Sing for the axe, with the iron crown,
  · And its edge of shining steel !
In the hands of the hardy pioneer,
  How it makes the forest reel !
The palace towers, and the temple spires,
  And the thundering engine's frame,
And the plashing wheel, and the trusty keel,
  From its conquering labours came !

      Then sing for the axe, etc.


Sing to the axe, the gleaming axe !
  That swings with the sounding sweep !
And scares the wild beast from his lair,
  Whilst the lofty cumberers leap !
Hurrah for the axe ! tis the king of tools !
  May its conquests never cease ;
'Twas our father's blade in the feuds of yore ;
  'Tis ours in the reign of peace.

    Then sing to the axe, the gleaming axe !
      That swings with the sounding sweep !
    And scares the wild beast from his lair
      Whilst the lofty cumberers leap.

# NATIONAL AND HEROIC SENTIMENT.

## OUR FUTURE HOME.

AIR—"GILDEROY." (*Campbell's Sett.*)

HAIL land of many woods and streams!
    The far-born exile's home,
Thy dawning prestige proudly beams
    Where'er the mind can roam.
From iron-girdled Labrador
    To far Columbia's strand,
From Erie's bank to Hudson's shore,
    Hail freedom's future land !

Though densely dark thy forests wave
    O'er many a pathless wild ;
And thousand nameless rivers lave
    Where seldom sunbeam smiled.
Tho' savage tribes in barbarous horde
    Still shout in vengeful fray ;
A holier charm than spear or sword
    Shall soon their ire allay.

What though thy fairest prospects own
    Vicissitude and toil,
Though high the snow-king piles his throne
    Above thy icebound soil,—

H

When spring, with soft relaxing breath,
   Dissolves his boreal reign,
Hope, song, and verdure charm each path,
   And plenty crowns each plain.

Let neighbouring nations in their pride
   War's gory flag display,
O'er our loved land may peace preside
   With pure transcendent sway.
While manly independence glows
   In every patriot breast,
May every virtue freedom knows,
   Make all thy children blest.

Come heavenly justice, poise thy hand,
   Thy trusty balance wield ;
In every council in our land
   Thy throne and altar build.
Wherever culture tills the soil,
   Or commerce cleaves the main,—
The skilful brain, the arm of toil,
   Do thou its right sustain.

Oh hasten, heaven ! the hallowed reign
   Of unity and love,
When worth and wealth o'er hill and plain
   In kindred band shall move !
When man to man, o'er each broad clime,
   Shall friend and brother be ;
And science, with her light sublime,
   Shall 'lume from sea to sea.

## A HIELAND HAGGIS.

### A SENTIMENTAL DISH FOR MORAL EPICURES.

I DINNA' care how many ken' my nation or my
    breeding :
The scoff o' country, name or race, is scarcely worthy
    heeding ;
I've known some chiefs were born in caves,—the
    brood o' tinkler randies—
Wha own'd mair worth and common sense than
    palace fondled dandies.
CHORUS—" I'm just as Hielan' as the hills,
       And this my greatest brag is :
       Let him wha scorns a Hielan' name
       Just taste a Hielan' haggis."

My faither was nae vaunty duke, my mither was
    nae duchess,
They lived and fen'd by honest toil, and never
    glaum'd at riches ;
They pang'd my feet in hose and brogues, as soon's
    I learned to toddle ;
A plilabeg my hainches deck't, a bonnet blue my
    noddle.
       I'm just as Hielan' as the hills, etc.

Nae sloppy jaups o' scaldin' tea, nae flimsy foreign
    wastry ;
Were ever down my gullet cramm'd, nae sugar'd
    plum-bake pastry ;
Guid barley bannocks, whangs o' cheese wi' butter
    stuck thegither,
And crowdy steep'd in creamy milk I aye got frae
    my mither.
       I'm just as Hielan' as the hills, etc.

They trained me soon to hate deceit, and every
    practice knavish,
To scorn ilk Jewish Judas tricks, and every feeling
    slavish :
To speak and act with due respect to folk in every
    station,               [or nation.
And rev'rence every honest man, whate'er his creed
        I'm just as Hielan' as the hills, etc.

My mither strave wi' pious zeal to fortify my con-
    science
'Gainst a' the fause besetting wiles o' folly, vice and
    nonsense.
My faither too wi' counsel grave in glowing tones
    advised me,
To brand hypocrisy and cant, nae matter wha des-
    pised me.
        I'm just as Hielan' as the hills, etc.

They sent me early to the schule to learn some
    lallan reading,
Where soon I push'd in dolties den, some bairns in
    richer clieding,
I learn'd to spell and scribble too, without much
    kind palaver,             [shaver.
Till half by nature, half by force, I grew a tacty
  -      I'm just as Hielan' as the hills, etc.

So thus prepared, with ardent trust, on wide per-
    ambulation,
I've trod the soil o' many climes, in many an oc-
    cupation ;
By manual art, or mental poise, with moral pride to
    guide it,
I've ate the bread and quaff'd the draught by in-
    dustry provided.
        I'm just as Hielan' as the hills, etc.

With ready will I change my craft—and don the
    garb that suits it :
For which I thank my native wit, and carena wha
    disputes it,
I never ply the flatterer's fraise—ne'er beg, and
    seldom borrow        -        [to-morrow.
What providence withholds to-day, it may supply
        I'm just as Hielan' as the hills, etc.

I've mix'd the choir o' social life in many a jovial
    quarter,
And hob-a-nobb'd wi' better cheils than oft wore
    star or garter !
The proffer'd draught frae honour's hand, wi' honest
    pride I've drank it.
But ne'er was muzzled for a bore, nor tossed in
    folly's blanket !
        I'm just as Hielan' as the hills, etc.

I've piped my strains on hills and plains, where
    gleesome flocks were friskin,
I've measured lines wi' learned divines, and strode
    in sock and buskin !
I've toil'd mid civic smoke and din, I've tugg'd on
    briny Ocean,              [war's commotion.
And borne my country's banner up 'midst gory
        I'm just as Hielan' as the hills, etc.

My cousins south o' Tweed and Tyne : when
    foreign loons would skelp them,
I ne'er was laith in heart or hand, wi' dirk or gun
    to help them :
Tho' aft wi' rude ungratefu' jeer, in turn, they whiles
    might daunt me ;
I just forgave their silly spite—their bombast could-
    na daunt me.
        I'm just as Hielan' as the hills. etc.

To season out my country's dish, the relish strength
    and size o't,
I'll add another grain o' spice, that epicures may
    prize it ;
A Hielan'man adores his hame, and if he's forced
    to shield it ;
A claymore, frae a parritch-stick, he'll aye ken how
    to wield it.

        I'm just as Hielan' as the hills, etc.

## ST. ANDREW'S DAY.

*Respectfully addressed to the brethren of St. Andrew's
Society, Kircardine, at their Anniversary for 1873.*

OLD November bleak and hoary,
    Casts aside to-night his crown ;
Doffs his dappled regal vesture,
    Lays his sword and sceptre down.
Vanquished in the stormy conflict,
    Bravely, 'mid the strife he fell :
Let us pay him loyal homage,
    Ere we toll his dying knell.

Like a stern, but duteous father
    Who his children's merits knew ;
Like a king who prized his subjects
    For their fealty ever true ;
Grateful for our meek submission
    To his brief but rigid sway,
He, as dying gift, bequeath'd us
    Good St. Andrew's natal day.

He, the Baptist's early convert ;
    Earliest chosen of our Lord !

Brother of that stern Apostle
　　Who for Christ could draw his sword.
Good St. Andrew, whom the abbot
　　Brought embalmed, across the sea,
From his tomb in far Byzantium,
　　Scotia's patron saint to be !

He—the saint whose sacred teachings
　　Earliest shook the Pagan shrine,
Burst the folds of heathen darkness,
　　Shedding Christian light divine.
Not a pompous mitred prelate,
　　Armed with Rome's presumptive pride ;
But the fisher of Bethsaida—
　　He at Patra crucified.

We, though far from where his relics
　　Lie entomb'd in Scottish mould,
Still his birthday rites can cherish,
　　As our fathers did of old.
Time and distance, land and ocean,
　　Toil and grief may interpose ;
But the legends of our fathers
　　Let our memories never lose !

We are Scots, and Scotsmen's offspring,
　　Sons of patriotic sires—
Sires whose deeds of noble daring
　　Sound from Freedom's loftiest lyres !
As to-night we roam in spirit
　　O'er yon hallowed land afar,
Let us prize their honoured footmarks
　　Bravely stamp'd in peace or war.

Scotia's scenes are all historic ;—
　　From her dells where coo's the dove
To her peaks, where screams the eagle ;—
　　Link'd to themes of awe and Love !

Far and wide, as thought, or vision
    O'er her record pores at will,
' Proud memorials of her valour,
    Power and genius greet us still.

Met to-night in bond fraternal
    Sacred pledges to renew,
Many a hallowed retrospection
    Opens to our mental view !
Fill your horns at memory's fountain !
    Scotia's fame a bumper craves ;
Though her soil we ne'er may tread on,
    'Tis her banner o'er us waves !

Pledge the heathery glens of Albyn
    Where the circling corrie leaps !
Where the deathless songs of Ossian
    Echo thro' the rocky steeps !
There the pibroch's martial numbers
    Roused the kilted clans of yore,
Up to Liberty's dread battle,
    Armed with targe and broad claymore !

Pledge her bens where Celtic bravery
    Kept at bay the power of Rome ;
Where the ruthless Norse invader
    Sought a throne, and found a tomb !
Boldly midst the strife of ages
    O'er the clouds, their summits tow'r !
Freedom's stronghold's built by Nature,
    Types of grandeur and of power !

Pledge the fair far-spreading Lowlands,
    Where the Doric muses rove
O'er the gowan-spangled meadow,
    Thro' the cool resounding grove !
There the field where mighty Wallace
    Quelled the vaunt of Southron pride !

Fields where Bruce, her rights defending,
  Scotia's Freedom ratified !

Pledge the rural scenes, of Coila,
  Hallow'd by her ploughman's fame !
And the "busky braes" of Ettrick
  With her minstrel Shepherd's name !
Stanley Shaw, and Green Gleniffer,
  Where in chaste melodious thrill,
Flowed affection's sweetest ditties
  In the strains of Tannahill !

Bonnie Tweedsdale, rich in story,
  Rich in bravery and in song ;
And the weird old haughs of Yarrow ;
  Oh ! what spells to them belong !
Not what Fancy robes in fiction,
  Deeds sublimer far I wot ;
Stir us in the lyre of Leyden,
  Charm us in the lays of Scott !

Scotia, land of bard and hero !
  Land of martyr, saint and sage !
Towering high in moral grandeur,
  Proudest realm on History's page !
Pledge her ancient hoary landmarks,
  Shrines of early power, and faith !
Gracing still her matchless landscapes,
  Braving Time's corrosive breath !

Pledge her treasured old traditions—
  Fruitful source of Minstrel's song !
And her modern social status—
  Purest earth's proud realms among !
Pledge the high-toned independence
  Of her sons and daughters leal—
Moral virtue, lore and genius,
  Mental power, and Christian zeal !

Raise our anthem !—" Rule Brittania,"
    Swell the vocal torrent high !
Let our theme be British Union,
    Freedom, Love, and Loyalty !
Unity by time unshaken !—
    Freedom that lets men be men !—
Love by selfishness unsullied,
    Loyalty to Virtue's reign !

By these emblems on our banner,
    By that motto stern and brave,
Let us shield our country's honour
    Whilst its folds above us wave !
Swell the patriotic chorus
    Till Ontario's wildwoods thrill !—
Let each birthday of St. Andrew
    Tell we're Scots and Britons still !

## CANADIAN VOLUNTEER'S CAMP SONG.

Arouse 'ye sons of British sires,'
    Heroes famed in ancient story ;
Wake again those inborn fires
    That lit of yore their path to glory ;
Up ! her holy cause again,
Freedom calls us to sustain.

Come ! for o'er yon border tide
    Band on band our foeman muster ;
Panther-like their legions hide,
    Couch'd within each brakey cluster !
Hungering, thirsting for their spoil :
Brave Canadians guard your soil.

Our broad land of wood and lake :
    Our dear won soil of Independence !

Our homes, our altars are at stake
 To gloat the ire of ruffian vengeance ;
Our hopes, our heritage to shield ;
On ! Celt and Saxon, to the field.

" Who that bears a Briton's name—
 " Who that owns a Briton's spirit :
" Justly proud of Britain's Fame,
 " Moral worth, and noblest merit ;
" Would not brave in danger's hour,
" Britain's foeman's deadliest pow'r ? "

We are Britain's eldest born—
 Should we to her cause prove traitors,
History's page would link, in scorn,
 Our names with frenzied conspirators,
And brand us with the ingrate's blot
Who shared his love, but own'd it not !

Lo ! the squire his dame forsakes,
 Scorning pride and dalliant trifle ;
Lo ! the woodman drops his axe,
 And in lieu takes up his rifle ;
Fast they move in valour's art,
When all are heroes at the heart.

Mount the courser, bare the brand,
 Swell the trumpet's brazen volume !—
Vandal hordes menace our land :—
 Quickly form in martial column,
Wave the banner, roll the drum,
Citizen and peasant come !

Charge the rifle, couch the lance,
 Waft the cannon to the border ;
Sons of Albion, Erin, France,
 Forward march ! in martial order :

Forth from hut, and forth from hall,
Patriot men are brothers all.

Let them come if come they must,
   Britain's sons will ne'er degrade her ;
True to all a mother's trust
   We'll repel each fierce invader ;
Or give as erst our fathers gave,
Alike a gibbet or a grave.

When the clang of hostile fray
   Loud o'er flood and forest rattles,
Highest midst the stern array
   Shall wave our " flag of many battles ! "
The banner which our fathers bore
Unsoiled, as in the fields of yore.

## DONAGHADEE.

### AIR—" DIRGE OF CARO'AN."

WHEREVER my home in the wild world may be,
My heart's in old Ireland, away o'er the sea,
'Mong the green sunny hills that look down on the
   stream,
And the soft dewy valleys that gladden'd youth's
   dreams ;
Where shelter'd in peace in the deep willow glen
I've listen'd the notes of the wild, merry wren,
And thought, in my fondness it warbled to me
" Sing beauty, sing love, and sing Donaghadee ! "

My breast has an aching—I cannot tell how,
But it felt not in boyhood the way it feels now :

And my brain too, has throbbings as well as my
  breast,
Which the wealth of an empire could ill set at rest.
There's a winter iu Nature, that falls on my heart,
Ere the hopes of the spring-tide can fairly depart;
And I still hear a small bird that whispers to me—
"Sing beauty, sing love, and sing Donaghadee!"

Ah, me! shall I never return, o'er the main,
To my home, in the north of old Ireland again?
Where the cot of my fathers for ages hath stood
Unstained by dishonour—unravaged by feud;
Where she—my fair Nora, my life's proudest joy,
'Neath the green mossy turf of the valley doth lie,
'Mongst the wild pretty flow'rs where she often with
  me
"Sang beauty, sang love, and sang Donaghadee!"

I love thee, my country! how fondly and true,
No realm in the wide world, so dearly as you,
Tho' tyrants oppress thee, and cowards beguile,
And the star of thy freedom seems clouded the while;
Yet, deep in my bosom, one solace I own,
'Tis the hope that thy day of misfortune hath flown,
And a little bird near me, proud-perch'd on a tree
"Sings beauty, sings love, and sings Donaghadee."

---

## THE CALL OF THE BARDS.

A song for the hundredth birthday of Robert Burns.—Not
written for a prize of fifty pounds.

### AIR—"HAIL TO THE CHIEF."

SING Brothers, sing, of the Minstrel of Coila,
  Loud be your songs in the life of his fame!

Hie with your harps to the shrine of his glory,
  Where Scotia invites, to exult in his name.
      Hie to the banks of Doon,
      Where many a sylvan tune,
Breathed from his lyre, on the echoes langsyne,
      Down where the winding Ayr,
      First claimed his muse's care;
Hie with your song gifts to hallow his shrine.

Ye who with breasts fraught with fond emulation,
  Toil for such meed as awaits him to-day;
Join in the might of your soul's approbation,
  The homage that genius demands us to pay.
      Come from your heathy Bens,
      Bards of the Highland Clans!
Lowlanders, Saxons and Cambrians, all:
      Druids of Erin green,
      Hasten to grace the scene;
String high your *Clarshechs* and hie to the call.

Tho' sever'd afar from thy bosom maternal,
  Thy sons Caledonia, the wide world may roam,
They can joy in that joy with the feeling faternal,
  That swells in the hearts of thy children at home.
      What Caledonian child,
      Worth loving tho' exiled,
Roams not in spirit to Coila to-day,
      Deep lodged in pathless wood,
      Haggard with solitude?
Home visions sacred, his musings can sway.

Far in the East where their battle din's roaring;
  Far in the South where they're mining for gold;
Far in the North, icy regions exploring;
  Far in the West midst the forest's dark fold.
      Woo'd by his social song,
      Charm'd by his wit so strong;

Sooth'd by his kindly theme—stirred by his ire,
    Proudly they breathe his name—
    Nought may gainsay his fame :
World wide his honours raise, Lord of the Lyre !

His was no pander muse, venal or craven,
    Flush'd by the smiles of Pride, chill'd by his frown,
Sternest adversity's baleclouds while braving,
    The meed of the servile he learned to disown.
      Down in a flowery dell,
      Love with its warmest spell,
Led him at gloaming to hymn in its praise ;
      Friendship and Freedom's joys,
      Nobly his soul could poise,
Warm midst the social choir, sounded his lays.

Patriots ! his song be your watchword for ages,
    Bold bard and brave !—to Humanity dear ;
Time pampered Tyranny quails o'er his pages,
    For time but reveals him the Bard and the Seer.
      Born 'neath yon roof straw,
      True priest of Nature's law,
Tremble ye strongholds of Prelate and King,
      Quake whilst with loud acclaim,
      Earth shouts in Robin's fame !
Nature's far shore with his Birth anthem ring.

## BONNIE LOCHGAIR.

Ah, I wish I were over by bonnie Lochgair,
Mang scenes where I fear I maun wander nae mair,
Mang the heather clad fells and the green bracken
    dens,
And the sylvan delights o' the wild Hielan' glens,

Whar the eagle soars high to the welkin sae blue,
And the wee lav'rock nestles amang the clear dew,
Whar the rude shelvin' rock guards the deer in his
    lair,
Mang the stern native wildwoods by bonnie Loch-
    gair.

But far, far away o'er the foam bursting tide
O' the dreary Atlantic, sae deep and sae wide ;
'Midst the lane dreary forests that shadow the West,
I maun pine wi' this strang love o' hame in my
    breast ;
I maun lie down by nicht on my pillow o' pain,
And wake to fresh anguish at morning again ;
Nae kindred endearments to saften my care,
Sae far frae the hame-haunts o' bonnie Lochgair.

I hear nae the sound o' the pibroch at e'en.
And I see nae the gowans that glanced on the green,
I hear nae the roar o' the steep waterfa',
Nor the corn-craik that waken'd the morn wi' his ca';
But hatefu' and eerie the grey howlet screams,
And the scowl o' a nichtmare aye burdens my
    dreams ;
To me nocht on earth can gie joy ony mair,
Sae far frae the lov'd haunts o' bonnie Lochgair.

Oh had I the art o' the happy sea-gull,
By times I wad soar and by times I wad scull,
Wi' pinions sae strang the fierce tempest I'd brave,
Or perch me to rest on the high rolling wave ;
Wi' eye proudly fix'd on the gate o' the dawn,
I'd skim o'er the ocean and strain for the lan',
Till soul-draughts o' freedom wi' Nature I'd share
Mang her stey mountain glories by bonnie Lochgair.

## BENEATH THE ROSE.

THERE's room enough in Canada, for men o' ony
  size !
Altho' their feet were acre braid, their heads as
  heich's the skies !
There's rowth o' wood and water baith to cook their
  bread and brose,
But there's something still a wantin' in't, that " lies
  beneath the Rose."

There are bonnie birds in Canada, as bonnie's
  earth can own,
Wi' plumes o' rainbow loveliness, and notes o' sil-
  lery tone ;
But they canna sing like British birds, and why !
  wad ye suppose ?
There's something absent frae their hearts, that
  "lies beneath the Rose."

There are winsome dames in Canada, leal, sonsie,
  brisk and braw,
Whase smiles might thowe an avalanche o' Green-
  land's cauldest snaw,
They've fouth o' bloom and hinnied looks—Guid
  sen' them honest Joes ;
But their's aye some grace they might improve,
  that "lies beneath the Rose."

There are Patriot Bards in Canada, but tame, tame
  are their lays,
Shorn o' inspired sublimity, like dulcets in a haze ;
Some chord is wanting on the lyre, 'tis hence the
  discord flows—
It wants the bauld heroic thrill that rings "beneath
  the Rose."

I

There are guid men in Canada, o' ilka craft we ken,
To guide the helm o' Kirk or State, or wield the
        plough or pen,
To swing the axe, or ply the spade, or fecht our
        braggart foes,
But there's something still a wanting in't that "lies
        beneath the Rose."

There are braw braid fields in Canada, if they o'
        stumps were free,
And till'd like ither nation's fields, and fenced as
        they should be,
There's rowth o' heat and moisture too, to foster a'
        that grows,
But there's something aye a wanting here, that
        "lies beneath the Rose."

There are braw braid lakes in Canada, wi' river
        links between,
Where commerce wi' increasing sails frae year to
        year is seen ;
Heaven prosper long her peacefu' coast, and ward
        invasion's blows ;
There is meikle, meikle wanting there that "lies
        beneath the Rose."

Now note the moral o' my sang—gin ye wad thrive
        at hame,
Ne'er scoff ye'r wise auld minnie's rule, nor o' her
        care think shame ;
Ye yet may need her helping han', how sune no
        prophet knows,
But there's aye maist smeddum in the heart that
        beats " beneath the Rose."

## OUR OWN BROAD LAKE.

LONG pent in wintry gloom so drear,
When neither sight nor sound could cheer ;
I've sigh'd to greet the spring-tide hours,
When leaves and blooms rebusk the bow'rs ;
To hear the cheerful matin lay
Of birds that mount the early spray,
Or mark what golden glories shake
Their radiance o'er " Our own broad Lake."

To feel the genial western breeze,
To list the hum of happy bees ;
To trace the flow'ret's early birth
When sunbeams dance in twinkling mirth ;
Each shady fold, each verdant scene,
Each dimpling brook's umbrageous screen
With all the varied joys that wake
In concert by " Our own broad Lake."

It comes ! the sun ascends our zone !
May, sparkling, mounts her gleaming throne ;
On every hand the groves resound,
And vernal grandeur peers around ;
Earth's teeming vision throbs in bloom
And every Zephyr breathes perfume,
Whilst gladsome lambs, in fold or brake,
Sport gaily by " Our own broad Lake."

Lo ! Huron free from winter's chain
Bursts gently on its shore again !
Its limpid wavelets tinkling clear
Delight the eye and charm the ear !
Its tressell'd banks in foliage green,
With light and shade enhance each scene,
And rustling murmurs quaintly make
Sweet music by " Our own broad Lake."

Hark ! as the woodman's vigorous blow
Fast lays the cumb'rous forest low,
The crack'ling log-pile's towering blaze
Ascending dims the noontide rays ;
The ploughman, shouting, guides his team,
The lowing heifer wades the stream,
And art and industry awake
Their hum around " Our own broad Lake."

And lo ! where o'er its breast serene,
Shines forth yon visionary scene !*
Yon phantom landscape, changing still,
Ignoring arts descriptive skill !
Tow'rs hamlets, cities, streams and woods,
All limned on the mirror clouds,
Romance's fav'rite haunt do make
The bosom of " Our own broad Lake."

Thus placid oft at night's still noon,
It sleeps beneath the cloudless moon,
Till envious of its dreamy rest,
Some power electric probes its breast ;
Then, wildly surging heave its waves,
And hoarse its voice of fury raves ;
And lightnings flash, and thunders quake
Sublimely o'er " Our own broad Lake."†

Hail Huron ! queen of beauteous floods !
Thy fertile banks and echoing woods ;
In peace, thy cities fair arise,
And white-sailed commerce o'er thee plies !
The bending keel—the dipping prow
Thy noble prestige can avow;
And future bards thy theme shall take
And proudly sing " Our own broad Lake."

---

* A Mirage.        † A Magnetic storm.

# A CELTIC CHIEFTAIN'S ADDRESS TO
# HIS CLAYMORE.

As every stanza bears reference to some well-known and
well-authenticated episode in Scottish history, the author
begs leave to inform the reader that the panegyric on his
country's glorious old war-blade is not the off-spring of a
romantic fancy, but a condensed picture of its widely-scat-
tered conquests long ago, endorsed by the most enlightened
readers of the present as well as bygone ages.

COME forth from thy scabbard, broad sword of the
      north !
I'll tell of thy deeds in the wars of the brave,
Since the rude Scandinavian sea-hordes came forth,
      Our sires and our country of yore to enslave.
First, then, may story tell how the invader fell
      Ghastly and grim on the strand of the heath,
Ever victorious, never inglorious,
      Proudly I pluck thee again from thy sheath,
          Claymore of Albyn !

High on those hills with their summits of blue ;
      Deep in those glens where the swift torrent rages ;
Far 'neath yon billows where screams the sea mew ;
      Pent in the mute murky silence of ages ;
Down with the nameless dead, stretch'd by thy
      gleaming blade,
Sank in their pride the tall chiefs of the sea ;
Still here thy hilt I touch : leap forth to greet my
      clutch !
Life's battle's o'er with them—not so with thee,
          Claymore of Albyn !

Yon green isle of spears, when the peace of its shore,
      By the war-cloud of Lochlin was darkened of old,
Can tell of thy prowess, when Fingal went o'er
      With his heroes of Morven, the stalwart and bold ;

Dark rolled the gory flood, thick as by tempest
    strew'd,
  Proud forms and haughty lay stiff on the plain ;
Bright brand, by Ossian grasp'd, thus in my hand
    when clasp'd,
  Despots may quail, as thou gleamest again,
        Claymore of Albyn !

When haughty Romagna her eagle displayed,
  And earth's proudest dynasties crouch'd to her
    laws,
Nor bribery, nor cowardice tarnish'd thy blade ;
  'Twas fashioned for freedom, and true to its cause;
Flashing from heathy ben, dashing from brakey
    glen,
  Prone as a meteor thy message was sped ;
Strong walls from sea to sea, tell how Rome dreaded
    thee ;
  Patriot weapon ! to glory thou'rt wed !
        Claymore of Albyn !

When the Saxon usurper, with stealthier pace,
  O'er Anglia strode in his gory career,
Indignantly scorning the weight of his mace,
  The tramp of his courser, the thrust of his spear;
Blazing Crantara's light, rousing the clansmen's
    might,
  Shook thy broad flash from each summit of flame ;
Freedom's staunch battle-brand, then in stark Ken-
    neth's hand,
  Gavest thou to Scotland a crown and a name,
        Claymore of Albyn !

When savage in purpose and lawless and stern,
  The chiefs of the Isles in their fury came o'er,
By conquest a regal Dominion to earn,
  Infesting each stronghold from centre to shore ;

Fast forth from glen and scar burst Alpine's clans
    to war,
    Swift as their native floods rush to the sea,
Sweeping their ruthless foes down with such lusty
    blows
    As no war-blade bestows equal to thee,
        Claymore of Albyn !

From his lairs in the south, o'er the Tweed and the
    Tyne,
    In his regal maraudings the lion oft prowled ;
But our hardy old fathers as oft made him whine
    By a feint of thy edge, wheresoever he growled ;
What though by Carronside Graeme and stout Stuart
    died,
    Guarding those rights a *Monteith* crouch'd to
    sell;
Nobly our Wallace brave, poising his mighty glaive,
    Righted our wrongs by thy foe-dreaded spell,
        Claymore of Albyn !

Chieftain of Ellerslie ! Martyr of Liberty !
    Wallace, the noble, the gifted and strong !
Where beats the patriot-heart, thrills not at name
    - of thee ?
    Shield of thy Caledon ! pride of her song !
Dragged to a traitor's doom—emblemless dark thy
    tomb—
    Who would not kiss the broad brand thou didst
    wave ?
Come forth thou cherished steel ; here at thy hilt I
    kneel !
    Ward of our heritage! sword of the brave !
        Claymore of Albyn !

Wild rode red ruin athwart our reft soil,
    Where jealousy captioned and tyranny trode,

Whilst the chiefs of the south raged like wolves on
    their spoil,
  Profaning the altars of freedom and God !
Till Frissel uplifting thee, Sword of Heaven's gifting !
  To Roslyn, the trusty of Caledon led ;
Burst bars of tower and keep : one wild tumultuous
    leap
  Wreathed thee in trophies that never can fade,
        Claymore of Albyn !

Bleeding, but unsubdued, wreck'd oft by local strife,
  Taunted by insolent Anglican pride,
Hoodwinked by traitor's guile, bartering our nation's
  Dashed by adversity's pitiless tide.        [life,
Loudly our country's voice rose in her leader's choice;
  Promptly responding the chief sought the field :
Southern vaunt back to turn—waved thee at Ban-
    nockburn,
  Liberty's harvest, when Bruce did thee wield,
        Claymore of Albyn !

Densely o'er Flodden the pall of the past
  Hath rolled its dark shadow, unscattered by time,
When nation to nation the gauntlet had cast,
  And both to the field brought their valour and
    prime ;
Hero with hero grasp'd—dead but yet firmer clasp'd,
  Sword crossed with sword lay encrusted in gore;
Ruin stood umpire by, grinning remorselessly,
  Claiming the field when the conflict was o'er,
        Claymore of Albyn !

Long though the yew-tree hath shaded the tomb,
  And long though the green cairn hath studded
    the plain,
Lo, Unity's day-star awakes from the gloom,
  And love, light and liberty triumph again !

Here rose a Percy's grave—there sleeps a Douglas
  brave !
Roses and thistles may bourgeon between :
Friendship of chivalry, virtue and bravery,
  O'er thy achievements enraptured I lean,
      Claymore of Albyn !

Sword of my country ! though ages of dread
  Have swept o'er the dynasties form'd by thy power,
In war, never dastard could sully thy blade,
  In peace, never heart that could trust thee need
      cow'r ;
Langside, where Celtic blood freely for Mary flowed;
  Shows where each phalanx the onslaught sus-
      tained,
Warding her queenly fame—guarding her diadem,
  Bravely our fathers thy prestage maintained,
      Claymore of Albyn !

These caves, which were temples, and altars those
  hills,
  When red persecution our fathers did chase ;
These rocks that now echo the songs of the rills
  Bear etchings of thine which time may ne'er
      efface.
Faith's valiant martyrs there, vigil-worn, kept thee
  bare ;
  Bible and broadsword their bulwark and tower ;
Bilboa and scabbard light, well might grace Carpet
  Knight—
  Thou worest no muffling in danger's dark hour,
      Claymore of Albyn !

Cleaver of helmets and shatterer of lances,
  Thou need'st no fiction to heighten thy fame !
For loftiest deeds ever told in romances
  With thine if compared were ignoble and tame.

What though in conflict rude oft urged by local
    feud,
  Dire seem the traces that dapple thy story;
Swung by a patriot's arm, nerved by the pibroch's
    charm,
  Where speaks the base deed that e'er dimm'd thy
    glory?
           Claymore of Albyn!

Firm as the pine on the crags of Ben Lomond
  Stands while the tempest around it doth rair,
So stands Clan Gregor the shock of the foeman,
  With might that can conquer and heart that can
    spare.
History restores a name long cancelled by defame;
  Worth has a life-germ no blight can destroy;
Inversnaid's talisman! reft chief and suffering clan
  Woke thy renown in the hand of Rob Roy,
           Claymore of Albyn!

Peerless in courage, in purpose oft erring,
  Our monarchs their claim oft asserted by thee; ·
Till bloodthirsty Cumberland's mission unsparing,
  Entombed their last hope on Culloden's red lea.
Still to lost royalty clinging with loyalty
  Long and devotedly wander'd our sires,
Sharing the exiles' lot, spurning each craven plot,
  Giving thy fame to earth's loftiest lyres,
           Claymore of Albyn!

Guardian of human rights!   O'er the deep waves,
  Wherever oppression would rear his dark throne,
Thy flash, striking terror to tyrants and slaves,
  Reveal thy high mission to earth's farthest zone.
Where fiery Gallia's breath, where sterner Russia's
    wrath,
  Where mad Hispania's torch fires the war-flame,

Where Ind or Turcoman shout in aggression's van,
  There art thou ready their rapine to tame,
      Claymore of Albyn !

Loudly the cannon's mouth belches its thunders forth;
  Cities and citadels crumble to dust ;
Who mounts the yawning breach, firm while the
      rocking earth
  Reels with the war surge from centre to crust ?
They, Albyn's conquering band, far from their native
      land,
  Fearless and foremost—each waving his steel ;
Death's missiles—shell and shot—thick as hail stay
      them not
  Saving thy spoils for humanity's weal,
      Claymore of Albyn !

Moulder of empires! may wisdom direct thee ;
  Framer of laws! be pure justice thy aim ;
Tamer of tyrants! let monarchs respect thee,
  And peace, love, and commerce increase with thy
      fame ;
Who with malignant taunt ; who with bravado vaunt,
  Dares to impugn the proud cause thou wouldst
      guard ?
Gleaming in ire how grand, swayed by a patriot's hand,
  Worth still can wreathe thee in glory's reward,
      Claymore of Albyn !

## HEATHERBELLS.

HEATHERBELLS ! heatherbells !
  They're the flow'rs I lang to see ;
A' the bloom o' foreign dells,
  Wi' my fancy winna gree.

Gie me Caledonia's flow'rs,
Glist'ning on her mountain towr's,
A' the sweets o' foreign bow'rs,
    Tame and tasteless blaw to me.

Heatherbells ! Heatherbells !
    Wavin' owre the craigie steeps,
Danglin' frae the dizzy fells
    Whaur the earn his vigil keeps.
Twinin' roun' the wild aik tree,
Whaur the rose wad pine and dee ;
Smilin' in their simple glee,
    Whaur the foamin' torrent leaps.

Heatherbells ! heatherbells !
    Rustlin' down the sylvan dens,
Whaur the echoes frae their cells
    Wauken to the shepherd's strains,
Whaur the tumblin' burnie roams,
Whaur it sleeps, and whaur it foams,
By the peacefu' Hielan' homes,
    Shelter'd deep in Freedom's glens.

Heatherbells ! heatherbells !
    Every charm o' life's young day
Binds my heart wi' weirdlike spells,
    Time can never chase away
Far, on fancy's pinions free,
Wafted owre the braid deep sea,
Roams my spirit, in its glee,
    Whaur the heatherbells do play.

Heatherbells ! heatherbells !
    Mountain gems o' glorious bloom ;
Mony a patriot legend tells
    How you've graced the hero's plume—
Nodded high on kingly crest,
Shimmer'd sweet on queenly breast,

Faulded saft in lane lown rest,
  Holy martyr in his tomb.

Heatherbells! heatherbells!
  Vainly search I bank and broo;
No' the simplest token tells
  Any spot whereon ye grew.
Ither Caledonian flow'rs
Whiles may glint in biels and bow'rs,
But thro' life's remaining hours
  Never mair I'll gaze on you.

---

## SONG.

### AIR—"MY AULD GUID WIFE."

THO' fair and fertile are the plains,
  The woodlands green and grand;
And bright the sparkling lakes and streams
  Of proud Ontario's land.
Tho' wealth and pleasure crown each toil,
  And all her soil is free,
There lies a land beyond the main,
  That's dearer far to me.

CHORUS—My native isle, my sea-girt isle!
        Weird realm of boyhood's glee;
      With deathless love, where'er I rove,
        I sigh and sing for thee.

Land of the towering mountain peaks
  That mock the tempest's ire,
And wear their snowy wreaths in June,
  Despite the solar fire.

Land of the heathy bens and braes,
   And deep resounding vales,
That ring response to winter's storms
   And summer's glowing gales.
          CHORUS—My native isle, etc.

Land of the frowning rocky scars,
   The pine and hazel glades,
Where modest worth and patriot love
   Are fostered in their shades;
· Where castled craigs, and cairny plains
   Their silent records bear,
Of deeds which history fails to tell,
   And what our fathers were.
          CHORUS—My native isle, etc.

Brave Albion ! land of many spells,
   The simple and the wild,
In dreams of thee I still can joy,
   As when I was a child.
The blight of years may scathe my form,
   And press my heart with care,
But ne'er can break one filial tie,
   Entwined in childhood there.
          CHORUS—My native isle, etc.

## No. I.

### SUBSTITUTE LAUREATE'S ODE

FOR THE INAUGURATION OF THE NEW DOMINION
OF CANADA.

I.

LIFT high the nation's song-charg'd voice;
   Our glorious advent proudly hail,
With loud acclaim let all rejoice,
   Till rapture sounds on every gale;

From city, forest, lake and river,
   Let jubilation shouts ascend—
Britannia's hand hath sealed forever,
   Th' bond, no nation's power can rend.


II.

Up ! sons of freeman : heirs of worth !
   Ours the broad land of wood and stream ;
Lo, earlier favour'd realms of earth,
   Shrink 'neath its star's ascendent gleam :
Its lines to light and love are given,
   Its prestige with the nobly free ;
Fair fostering in the smiles of heaven,
   Its fields expand from sea to sea.


III.

Unroll the banner of our sires,
   The standard of the truly brave,
Whose fame is wed to loftiest lyres,
   O'er every clime and every wave.
On citadel, and tow'r and temple,
   High the lov'd gonfalon raise ;
Beneath its folds so pure and ample,
   Wake all our hopes of future days.


IV.

To-day an empire vast and fair,
   Transmits its name to history's page,
Which, nobly and enduring there,
   Must rise in fame from age to age ;
Ever in power and worth increasing,
   Secure from dark despotic sway,
Adorn'd by every earthly blessing,
   'Lumed by religion's brightest ray.

### V.

Whilst tyrant dynasties of earth,
   In gory ruin, tottering fall,
Lo, our Dominion leaps to birth;
   'Tis her's the crown, and their's the pall.
Call forth the joy of patriot bosoms,
   Wake the full choir of minstrel song,
Whilst summer wreathes earth's brow with blossoms,
   And echo shouts her cells among.

### VI.

Ours be the reign of love and peace,
   Our weapons not with carnage stained,
We triumph o'er no martyr'd race,
   Nor waste the blood of tribes enchained;
The bloodless war which virtue wages,
   Is not with deadly sword or spear,
Yet fast the gloom of babarous ages
   Before its face must disappear.

### VII.

Call forth the city! wake the wild!
   Let wealth and labour join the train:
Let grandame hoar, and lisping child,
   Commingling swell the festal strain.
Shout ye dense woodlands! till Vancouver
   Responds to rugged Labrador,
And, "Rule Britannia! rule forever"
   Rings from the Pole to Erie's shore.

## CALEDONIA.

WHEN Nature first rear'd Caledonia's hills,
Wi' their stie tow'ring taps and their clear streaming
    rills,
She sought, 'mang the gems that to Flora belang,
For a wreath that should always be sacred in sang;
Nae saft downy lillies, nor bower roses vain,
Nae tame tender nurslings o' garden or plain
        But she chose the strang heather,
        The hardy, wild heather,
        The purple-bell'd heather,
        That waves on the bens.

The beauty, majestic in form and in hue,
Sublimely, her spells round their steep summits
    threw,
The rainbow's rath tints, and the clouds rolling gloom,
And the mirage that floats o'er the vale's misty womb,
Wi' a' the stern grandeur o' shadow and ray,
That fancy could wish for her story or lay.
        Amang the strang heather,
        The blooming wild heather,
        The purple-bell'd heather
        That waves on the bens.

Then liberty came on her wind-wafted car,
Wi' her patriot train, and her weapons of war;
And she built on the steeps where the cataracts fa',
The tow'rs o' her strength, and the shrines o' her law,
She roved in the chase, happy, fearless and free;
And she piped to rock-ringing echoes her glee,—
        Amang the brown heather,
        The bonnie wild heather,
        The purple-bell'd heather
        That waves on the bens.

K

Then honour came down frae the regions above,
Wi' her kindred companions, leal, friendship and
    love ;
And chose the retreats o' the dingle and glen,
In the lown biels o' peace ayont tyranny's ken,
Whar they nourish'd their offspring, the trusty and
    brave,
Wha ne'er bent to despot, the knee o' a slave,
        Amang the strang heather,
        Their native brown heather,
        The purple-bell'd heather,
        That waves on the bens.

Lang ages hae pass'd ;—but the proud hills are
    there,
Still tow'ring in glory aloft in the air,
Wi' their mantles unsullied, in bloom o' their prime,
And their birthright o' freedom unshaken by time ;
They boast o' a future as well as a yore—
For valour still poises her mighty claymore.
        Amang the strang heather,
        The tough Hielan' heather,
        The purple-bell'd heather
        That waves on the bens.

Tho' lang—Caledonia—far o'er the sea,
A way-farer weary, I've wandered frae thee,
Not a' the allurements o' nature or art,
Could cancel thy claims as the home o' my heart :
And till death still its beatings, aye, sacred thou'lt
    be,
For my soul's sweetest visions are centred in thee.
        Amang the brown heather,
        The wild blooming heather,
        The purple-bell'd heather
        That waves on thy bens.

## THE AULD HILLS AT HAME.

COME join in my sang o' the auld hill's at hame,
For wha but feels proud o' their grandeur and fame?
O'er the high rolling clouds 'yond the force o' the
    storm,
How daring in aspect! how lofty in form!
They tow'r till their taps in the blue lift they hide,
In a realm where the earn his bauld pinions ne'er
    tried.
He's nae honest Scot, and deserves na the name,
That loes na to sing o' the auld hills at hame.

Stout warders o' freedom, how stalwart they stand,
The grace and the glory of Albion's land;
Wi' their wild dizzy clifts whaur the young eagle
    screams,
And their deep furrow'd glens whaur the loud tor-
    rent streams,
Wi' their girdles o' heather and garlands of broom,
That wave o'er the cairnies their tassels o' bloom;
Wha thinks on langsyne and his forbearers fame,
But justly feels proud o' the auld hills at hame?

In the lown o' their valleys where nature hath spread
A' her mingled attractions o' beauty and dread,
They shelter a race which in valour and worth
Has seldom been rivall'd by ony on earth.
Let history vaunt what its Spartans hae been,
But frae brave Fingal's days, till the days we hae
    seen,
Nae birthplace o' heroes the wide world can claim
Like that o' our clansmen, the auld hills at hame.

Since the rude Scandinavian rovers o' yore
For plunder or conquest invaded her shore,

Ilk strife-loving despot hath battled in vain
The freedom of Albion's sons to enchain;
They came frae the east in their galleys o' pride,
And they came frae the south, o'er the Tweed and
    the Clyde,
And they came frae the west, her proud prestige to
    tame,
But they aye failed to speil o'er the auld hills at
    hame.

And lang as the gleid o' our patriot fires
Can glow into flame at the deeds o' our sires,
And lang as the heather its red bells may shake,
'Mongst the crags where the pibroch the echoes
    can wake;
Ay! long as the cataracts foam down their steeps,
And prone thro' the valley the wild corrie sweeps,
Sae lang ilk true Scot may exult in their fame,
And joy in the sang o' the auld hills at hame.

## CLAVEN GLEN.

### AIR—"CRAIGIE LEA."

I LO'E the canty bubbling burn,
    That wimples down the rushie lea,
For in its sang there's aye a turn,
    That mak's its music dear to me.
I've paidlet in its silver tide,
    When childhood's cloudless hours were mine;
And pu'd the blossoms from its side,
    To busk my lassie's brow langsyne.
        The bonnie burn, the wimplin' burn,
           That sings in Claven's woody glen;
        Nae ither stream could soothe life's dream,
           Like that sweet burn in Claven glen.

'Twas no' that lordly taste had there,
 Begemm'd the soil wi' culture's skill;
Nor rear'd the glittering palace fair,
 To grace the greenwood skirted hill.
A prouder charm, a holier band,
 A grace which wealth could ne'er impart;
Was woven there by Nature's hand,
 And twined forever 'round my heart.
   The bonnie burn, the wimplin' burn, etc.

Its mossy margin saft and green,
 Its primrose banks so sweetly braw;
Its elfin shades o' wildwood screen,
 Still haunt my memory far awa'.
The robin's carol trembling clear,
 The blackbird louder in his glee;
The scented hawthorn, birk and brier,
 That formed loves' earliest bield to me.
   The bonnie burn, the wimplin' burn, etc.

Oh, happy youth! ilk kindly tie,
 Ilk sacred spell by glen and brae;
Within my bosom still defy,
 The envious blight o' time or wae!
Afar o'er many a distant scene,
 Beyond the ocean's heaving tide,
I've sigh'd and sung wi' tear-filled e'e;
 My native haunts, my bow'ry Clyde.
   And aye the burn, etc.

### No. 2.

## A SUBSTITUTE LAUREATE'S ODE.

WE now hae reason to be proud, and glad at heart,
  and a' that:    [sing, and a' that,
To toss our hats and cheer aloud, and leap and

And a' that, and a' that, and muckle mair than a'
 that;
Frae Britain's shore they've sent us o'er some dainty
 news, and a' that.

Ye ken we lang hae been abused, pimp-ridden,
 scoff'd and a' that,
And just like helpless step-bairns used, it wisna
 nice ava that :
E'en a' that, and a' that, and sometimes waur than
 a' that,
Some menseless loons in southron toons, our heritage wad claw that.

Our moral star seem'd on the wane, our social state,
 and a' that ;
Designing tools and arrant fools wrought waste and
 want, and a' that,
And a' that, and a' that—our trade and trust, and
 a' that,
In ruin's maw, for guid and a', seem'd swallow'd up
 and a' that.

Tho' many a sage prophetic chiel, wi' warning voice,
 and a' that,
Toil'd lang and sair to haud us leal in loyalty, and
 a' that,
For a' that, and a' that, there seem'd sma' hope for
 a' that,
For Yankee-doodle's didling arts hoodwink'd us
 aye, for a' that.

He tauld us that our British ties were slavish chains,
 and a' that ;
That Canada could never rise whilst link'd to
 crowns and a' that,

And a' that, and a' that, to titles, thrones an' a' that;
An' fostered up rebellious ire to open strife, an' a' that.

By many deep laid dastard wiles in friendly guise,
    and a' that,
He strave to lair us in his toils, and eke by force,
    and a' that,
E'en a' that, and a' that, our commerce crush'd, and
    a' that,
Gave guns and swords to Fenian hordes, to shoot
    and hack us sma' that.

But spite his frothy floss and spleen, hypocrisy, and
    a' that,
His bullying brag, and knavery mean, detraction,
    lies, and a' that,
And a' that, and a' that, tho' hard he tugg'd wi' a'
    that,
To rax us ower was past his pow'r : we're Britons
    yet, for a' that.

We've now obtained a nation's height, we're christ-
    ened too, and a' that,
And diel a stroke we had to fight, it came by na-
    ture's law that ;
And a' that, and a' that, a kingdom too, and a'
    that,
But, what will Yankee-doodle say when he's con-
    vinced o' a' that ?

We'll hae a monarch—king or queen, a sceptre,
    throne, and a' that,
And dukes, and earls, and knights I ween, and
    titles, mair than a' that,
Than a' that, and a' that, an army great, and a' that,
A navy strang, our foes to bang, on ocean, lake, and
    a' that.

Then high auld Britain's banner raise, loud peal
    your bells, and a' that,
Let bonfires blaze on a' your braes, and cannons
    roar, and a' that,
And a' that, and a' that, triumphant shout, and a'
    that,
Afar let fame the deed proclaim, and loud her
    trumpet blaw that.

## SONG TO IRELAND.

O ERIN, dear, beyond the sea,
    Fair country of my sires,
My fancy wrapt in dreams of thee,
    Still glows with youth's fond fires ?
For restless Memory's daring flight,
    Where'er my sojourn be,
With untired ardor, morn and night,
    Devoutly turns to thee.

Land of my early childhood's home,
    Where first, by grove and stream,
With ardent glee I learned to roam,
    And list the song-bird's theme ;
Where happiest, on the old school green
    I pranced in merriest plays,—
Oh ! would my life had always been
    As bright as schoolboy days !

O Erin, dear ! where tenderest love
    First warm'd my youthful breast ;
Where first, in hallow'd green-wood grove,
    Its passion I confessed ;

'Tho' fortune lured me from thy shore,
　To climes beyond the sea,
Still dearly in its warmest core,
　My bosom yearns for thee.

Land of the fertile flowery plains,
　And steep green sunny hills,
Where beauty's loftiest grandeur reigns,
　And freedom's harp yet thrills—
For tho' 'tis hushed in Tara's hall,
　And mute in Connor's tow'r,
The spell that holds its voice in thrall
　Is weakening every hour.

Loved Erin! land of sweetest song
　And eloquence sublime,
Of martial genius, skill'd and strong,
　Renown'd in every clime ;
For thine are Goldsmith's matchless lays,
　And classic Grattan's fire,
Thine glorious Wellington, whose praise
　Hath graced earth's loftiest lyre.

Fair Erin, dear! from 'yond the sea,
　A moan comes on the gale—
As if a nation, grand like thee,
　In Slavery's bonds did wail ;
If thraldom's virus thee enslaves,
　Why foster bigot zeal ?
If Albion's banner o'er thee waves,
　It waves to guard thy weal.

Green realm of legends wild and strange,
　And thrilling songs of yore,
How often doth my spirit range
　Thy scenes, from shore to shore !

By ruins grim, and caverns hoar,
    In quaint tradition shrined;
To revel 'midst the marvel lore
    That charm'd my youthful mind.

But, oh, my country! if thy wrongs,
    A sure redress demand,
Let moral valour burst the thongs,—
    Oh, sheathe the rebel's brand!
Shake from thy fold the vampire throng
    That sucks thy vital spring,
And soon shall liberty's proud song
    Thro' all thy echoes ring!


## TORRYBURN.

Torryburn's a bonnie place!
    Were ye e'er in Torryburn?
Mony a tie tae mem'ry dear
    Binds my heart to Torryburn.
Wi' fortune's rovin', random train,
I've travell'd far, o'er land an' main,
But aye my fancy turns again
    Tae couthie, dear, auld Torryburn.

No a stream Ontario owns,
    Clearer rins than Torryburn;
Ne'er a rural glen is there
    Sae green's the glen o' Torryburn.
There lauchin' Spring, wi' fairy han',
In daintiest flow'r gems busks the lan';
There first the laverock lits at dawn,
    Abune the dells o' Torryburn.

Brawly bloom the simmer braes
   Roun' the Links o' Torryburn.
Dear tae love 's the plantin' shades
   An' brākey holms o' Torryburn.
Ten thousand dangers wad I brave,
On mountain waste or briny wave,
My weary feet ance mair tae lave
   In blythsome, pure, auld Torryburn.

Richly harvest's gowden corn
   Cleids the straths o' Torryburn ;
Gaily rings the shearers' sang
   Amang the rigs by Torryburn.
Fair scenes o' peace an' pure content,
Whaur a' my happiest days were spent,
Tae mad ambition's wiles unkent ;
   How dear tae me was Torryburn !

Cauld tho' winter's driftin' snaw
   Wreathes the fells by Torryburn,
Caulder far's the stranger's hearth,
   Far awa frae Torryburn.
Nae mair I'd share ilk merry scene,
At Beltane tide or Hallowe'en ;
At Yule, when a' in glee convene,
   They'll miss me sair in Torryburn.

Fickle fortune !—'twas for thee
   I forsook fair Torryburn,
Kith an' kin, an' a' I lo'ed
   Dear as life, at Torryburn.
Oh ! grant ae wish—the last I'll crave—
Tae bear me o'er the Atlantic wave,
An' lay my banes in some lone grave,
   Beside my sires at Torryburn.

# MISCELLANEOUS PIECES, PATHETIC AND HUMOROUS.

## AN AULD MAID'S REMONSTRANCE.

AIR—"RUSTIC FELICITY."

WHAT can a lane body, what can a leal
    body,
        What can an auld body do for a
        man?
Nae charms to commend her, nae kin to be-
    friend her,
        Her ringlets turned lyart, her baffets turn'd
        wan.
Oh, dreary's the prospect that tends an auld
    maiden;
        Its cauld and its lanesomeness troubles
        ane sair,
As weel as the scaith and the callous up-
    bradin'
        O' gilpies I've nursed wi' a mitherly care.
            What can a lane body, etc.

Oh, dool on the wiles and the cantrips o' fashion,
    That fetter the younkers afore they can fen;
And mak' them the slaves o' a' fancifu' passion,
    A ban on the credit o' twascore and ten.
        What can a lane body, etc.

My mither aye taught me, wi' counsel maist zealous,
    To scorn a' the airts o' the giddy and vain,
To shun a' the lures o' the coaxin' young fellows ;
    Her maxim was aye, "*get a douce ane or nane.*"
       What can a lane body, etc.

I've wrought a' my days at the spinnin' and shearin',
    And thrave by my thrift 'twixt the woo' and the
       corn :
And aye, when a laddie my price cam a speerin',
    I bade him refrain till his beard could be shorn.
       What can a lane body, etc.

A' my auld cronies, my sisters and cousins,
    Afore ane-and-twenty contrived to get wed ;
But tho' I could reckon my offers by dozens,
    At twa score and twa I'm a lanesome auld maid.
       What can a lane body, etc.

When the rude storms o' the winter come roarin',
    Whirlin' the drift to my wee ingle cheek,
Sadly I hurkle in sorrow despairin',
    Comfort or kindliness whaur can I seek ?
       What can a lane body, etc.

Honest Mess John and his deacons sae pious,
    Tho' aye interested in bodies like me,
Its just for the wee pickle gear we've laid by us,
    To glaum't for the session as sune as we dee.
       What can a lane body, etc.

Aften I wish—tho' I'd modestly speak o't—
    To make a life bargain wi' some honest jo ;
For love I am sure he'd hae a' he could seek o't,
    And goupings o' gowd that wad mak' his heart
       glow.
       What can a lane body, etc.

Mightna some leal fallow, tho' ayont fifty,
  Tired, like mysel, o' his livin' alane,
Marrow his lot wi' a lass that's been thrifty,
  His credit to prop ere her bairn-time be gone?
    What can a lane body, etc

## MY AIN GUIDMAN.

AIR—THE RANTIN' ROARIN' HEILANMAN.

CHORUS—O send me hame my ain guidman,
        My leal guidman, my fain guidman;
        This weary war 's a woful ban,
        That twines the heart ands oul frae me.

O dool upo' the menseless pride
  That stains the warl' wi' gory war,
And bids deep oceans, roarin' wide,
  To sever lovin' hearts sae far;
For what to me is a' the gain
  Ambition claims ayont the main,
If a' the comforts ance my ain
  Are reft to prop its lofty plea?
      CHORUS—O send me hame, etc.

When I bethink me o' the days,
  Sae dearly prized, sae early gane,
When Kenmure's haughs and bonnie braes
  Held a' I proudly ca'd my ain;
I scarce can quell an angry pray'r;
  I canna hide my bosom's care;
It dings me maistly to despair,
  To listen e'en the lintie's glee!
      CHORUS—O send me hame, etc.

Wi' Jamie's plaid and *aiken crook*,
　　Upo' the hills his flocks I tend ;
And mony a lang and ruesome look,
　　Out o'er the foamin Solway send ;
But tho' I strain my aching sight,
　　Frae morn's pale daw' till dowie night,
Across its billows foamin' white,
　　Nae bark brings Jamie back to me.

CHORUS—O send me hame, etc.

I sit me by the auld grey cairn
　　Whaur first his love to me he tauld,
And hug our ae sweet laddie bairn
　　Close to my heart in couthie fauld ;
And gazin' in his dimplin' face,
　　Wi' a' a mother's pride I trace,
Ilk loesome line o' manly grace,
　　That made his dad sae dear to me.

CHORUS—O send me hame, etc.

Thou kindly power, wha's will can stay
　　The war-cloud, and the ragin' wave,
Oh ! hasten roun' the peacefu' day,
　　That yields me back my lo'ed and brave !
Ilk fauld and fell by hamely ken
　　Shall ring wi' mony a gratefu' strain,
And ne'er may war's rude call again,
　　Gar him forsake his native lea.

CHORUS—O send me hame, etc.

———

## AVOCA.

AVOCA, again in thy calm sheltered valley,
　　I woo the retreats by thy wild winding stream,

Where the fair summer flowers deck each rural alley,
  As mellowed in soft tints of twilight they gleam.
On the verge of the forest the pale aspens quiver;
  The dark-mantled cedar still shadows the dell ;
The meek-scented birch droops its folds o'er the
    river,
  Whose banks bear the moss-pink and lovely blue-
    bell.

'Twas here—when the sun o'er broad Huron retiring,
  In hues of rich grandeur embellish'd the grove,
Whilst nature's gay charms round my pathway ad-
    miring,
  I first owned the power and presence of love.
'Twas here—where love's star from the blue zenith
    beaming,
  First hallowed our tryst in the vine-tressel'd glade,
As with valour and truth in his warm bosom teeming,
  Young Henry first proffered his vows in the shade.

How sad now each scene, of his presence forsaken,
  Thy echoes are mute, or they sigh but in pain ;
His sweet voice no more shall their rapture awaken,
  His foot shall ne'er press thy green valley again,
For far 'mid the tumult of war's fell commotion,
  He sank where the bravest in battle did fall ;
They gave him a grave in the depths of the ocean,
  The winds sang his requiem, the waves were his pall.

But still, dear Avoca! thy stream in its wand'rings
  Can murmur response to my soul-cherished pain ;
I'll oft trace our haunts by its fitful meanderings,
  As oft sigh his name to thy zephyrs again.
I'll sit by the fountain and twine the green willow :
  His form my rapt fancy shall often restore ;
'Till calmly I'll sleep with thy moss for my pillow,
  Whence nature shall wake me to anguish no more.
    J.

## THE HARP OF LOVE.

THEY bid me cease to sing o' love,
    They ca't an outworn theme,
Unworthy o' the minstrel's lay :—
    A fause and fading dream !
But na—their notions a' are vain ;
    And cauld their hearts maun prove
That dinna beat the holy flame
    O' deathless heaven-born love.

I wadna hae my life bereft
    O' love's e'en simplest string,
Tho' wealth and fame as bribes they'd gie
    Life's venal lays to sing.
In fortune's circles proud and gay
    Let laurell'd hirelings prate ;
I can despise their tinsell'd strains,
    And scorn their servile state,

Gie me the woodlands dern and wild,
    The wide and blooming lea,
The craggy mountain's steep and stern,
    The clear streams rowing free !
The heathy fells, the ferny knowes,
    The lavrock's joy above—
A freeman's rank—a peasant's hame—
    A rustic lyre and love !

When Nature first my lyre bequeathed,
    To love's saft notes 'twas strung ;
And fondly beat my glowing heart,
    As o'er its tones I hung.
Wi' it I sought the echoin' dells,
    And found response was there,
And streams and flowers in wildest scenes
    Hae brichten'd to its air.

Altho' some desert cave unknown
  My destined hame should be ;
Whar mortal ear might never list
  My hermit minstrelsy ;
In nature's ear the theme I'd pour
  Whilk first she bade me sing,
And yield her back in death her lyre,
  Love tuned in every string.

## BESSIE ROY.

AIR—"WILLIE WAS A WANTON WAG."

NEAR Avoca blooms a maiden,
  Sweet as summer's fairest flow'r,
Tinged with morning's purest dewdrops,
  Nursed in beauty's softest bow'r.
In her eye the beam of dawnlight,
  On her lip the smile of joy,
Meek and mirthful play the dimples
  On the cheek of Bessie Roy.

      Bonnie blooming Bessie Roy,
        Winsome, happy Bessie Roy,
      Meek and mirthful play the dimples,
        On the cheek of Bessie Roy.

By yon streamlet blooms the lily,
  Chastest flow'r that decks the grove.;
But a chaster flow'r than Bessie
  Never graced the path of love.
Like a pearl in downy casket,
  Free from every base alloy,

Virtue's pure unsullied treasure
　　Gems the breast of Bessie Roy.

　　　Bonnie blooming Bessie Roy,
　　　　Winsome, happy Bessie Roy,
　　　Virtue's pure unsullied treasure
　　　　Gems the breast of Bessie Roy.

Fashion's gay voluptuous minions
　　Proudly flaunt in art's display,
Gilded moths that haunt the sunshine—
　　Changing hues in every ray.
Oh ! how vain their transient lustre !
　　Time their toil and art their toy ;
Native charms with grace enduring,
　　Gem the life of Bessie Roy.

　　　Bonnie blooming Bessie Roy,
　　　　Winsome, happy Bessie Roy,
　　　Nature's bloom and native pleasures
　　　　Gem the life of Bessie Roy.

Down Avoca's pleasant valley—
　　Free from fretful city strife,
Where the swain could not feel happy
　　With sweet Bessie for his wife?
Sculptured halls and pencilled graces
　　Never could his rest annoy ;
Blest by sweet Avoca's river,
　　Folding lovely Bessie Roy.

　　　Bonnie blooming Bessie Roy,
　　　　Winsome, happy Bessie Roy ;
　　　Blest e'en should he live forever,
　　　　Folding lovely Bessie Roy.

## CAULD GLOOMY FEBERWAR.

Of the following verses, the first four lines and the four last, are the production of Robert Tannahill; being all that remains of the original. I have taken the liberty of supplying the other stanzas, in the hope of carrying out what I suppose to be sentiments intended for filling up the outline. The air is "NEIL GOW'S STRATHSPEY."

THOU cauld gloomy Feberwar:
  O gin thou wert awa!
I'm wae to hear thy souchin' wins,
  I'm wae to see thy snaw:
I'm wae for a' the bieldless birds
  That chirp aroun' the lee:
They scarce can flap their dowie wings,
  And ken na whaur to flee.

Thou snell scowlin' Feberwar;
  What gars ye linger here?
There's nae music in thy voice,
  A lanely heart to cheer:
There's nocht of sunshine in thy sky,
  To woo the lark to rove
Up amang the gouden clouds,
  To chant her lay o' love.

Thou grim growlin' Feberwar!
  Thou gar'st me pine and greet;
Thy gaze has frozen ilka burn
  That wont to sing so sweet.
I lang for spring, wi' glowing rays,
  To cheer the woods forlorn;
And wauk gowan's dewy e'e
  Wi' pearly glance at morn.

Thou stern, ruthless Feberwar !
   An thou wert fairly gane,
What hopes and joys wad Nature bring,
   To mak' my bosom fain !
For my bonnie, braw young Hielander ;
   The lad I loe sae dear,
Has vow'd to come and wed me,
   In the spring time o' the year.

---

## THE AGE OF HORSE FLESH.

### A Satire.

#### AIR—"THE BRAES O' GLENORCHY."

Since time, ow're in Eden, his circuit began,
He has measured by ages the progress o' man :
There were ages o' *airn*, and o' *copper* and *lead*,
O' brass and o' siller, and goud, it is said !
When ae age wore out, he aye brocht roun' afresh—
And the ane we hae noo, is the "*age o' horse flesh* ;"
Depend on this maxim, and keep it in force—
Gif ye'd rise to distinction, you maun hae a horse.

A man may be thrifty—hae wisdom and airt,
Hae fouth o' guid lear, and a sound honest heart ;
His merits and virtues a' free frae defect ;
But, wantin' a horse, he can hae nae respect.
He may claw wi' his fingers, and scart wi' his taes,
For his wife and his bairns to get vittels and claes :
His toils a' rin' thrawart—frae bad aye to worse ;
But there's nane cares a fig, cause he ha'es na' a horse.

There are chiels that hae horses, wha ought to hae
    nane—
They do ither folks wark, and mislippen their ain:
They're far too obleegin' when needy folk ca',
And ken na the value o' horse flesh ava;
In spring time they plew and harrow their soil,
And neer charge a cent for their fother nor moil;
They leuk on sic acts as on duties, of course;
But I'd no be sae simple gif I had a horse.

Gif I had a horse, oh ! how proud I wad be !
The bouk o' my spirit the warl' soon wad see;
Nae mair on *shank's naigie* I'd paidle the mire,
Nor count mysel' second to nabob or squire !
I'd sit on a saddle, saft pachit wi' woo',
As stie as a general equipped for review;
Wi' braw tinsel trimmings weel fitted, of course,
I'd ride to some purpose gif I had a horse.

Gif I had a horse and a buggy sae neat,
Ye wad never fin' space in't for poverty's seat,
Nae lean draigled vagrant should sit by my side;
For wha wad keep horses that beggars might ride?
I ne'er deemed it proper to troke wi' the poor;
There's nae profit in't, and sma' credit I'm sure;
This worthy auld maxim I'd always indorse—
" *Let charity wintle*, gif I had a horse."

Gif I had a horse, Oh ! sic knowledge I'd hae,
There wad nane contradict me in ought I wad say;
A' my words wad be wit, a' my notions correct,
And the grist o' my judgement there's nane wad
    suspect.
I'd revel in friendship, and wallow in fame,
And hae some grand title affixed to my name !
But barren o' gumption, and credit of course,
I maun ever remain gif I haena' a horse.

Humpbackit King Richard, wha fought for a crown,
When at Bosworth defeated he fain would hae flown;
In his tumult o' terror, distraction and rage,
Whilst he pranced like a panther enclosed in a cage;
He bode a guid price for a naig on that day,
To bear his gnarled carcass awa' frae the fray;
He proffered his kingdom—'*twas England, of course,*
Which proves the high value he placed on a horse!

There's a substance which some thought a fable
    langsyne;
But its turned out a fact, and its truth I'll define:
Ye've heard o' the famous "philosopher's stane"
For which men o' science sic searchin' have ha'en;
It wad turn into goud ilka thing that it touched;
And some swapp'd their souls to be with it enrich'd.
What fools they, auld Beelzybub's bonds to indorse;
I'd prove you I'd found it, gif I had a horse.

The chiel wi' the horse, a' mankind count as brither,
And if he own ane he may soon own anither;
He's born to success, by reciprocal rule;
For we're a' prone to basting the belly that's full.
Yon auld simple proverb, there's truth in't ye'll fin',
That "*ae touch o' nature mak's a' the warl'd kin;*"
And "a touch o' horse flesh," will the sequel en-
    force—
I'd be up 'mang the great ones gif I had a horse.

## NELLIE ADAIR.

### AIR—"HARPER OF MULL."

FAR away from the turmoil of life's busy throng,
The sweet favoured home haunts of boyhood
    among;
How prone is my fancy to visit each scene,
Where my bosom's first raptures awakened have
    been !
Every flower on the mead—every bush in the
    glen,
Hath a charm for my heart, as endearing as then ;
Every spell that erst hallow'd my hope dreamings
    there,
When I strung pearly garlands for Nelly Adair.

Pure joy, robed in sunlight, danced gay o'er our
    path,
As together we roamed o'er the bloom-purpled
    strath !
Whilst the bee's tiny bugle, and burn's rushing
    sound,
The musical magic of love shed around.
Cold fate could not harm us—we lived but to be
Of each other a part, in a realm full of glee,
Where no echoes responded the murmurs of care,
As I strung flowery song wreaths for Nelly Adair.

I gazed on her fair face—I braided her brow,
On the burn's sloping brink, where the primroses
    blow ;
And the wealth of my soul was the truth of her
    breast,
As, warm in its throbbings, to mine it was pres't.

Long, long years have passed o'er the sweet homely
    vale,
Since our Eden was scatter'd by Death's blighting
    gale,
Still my fancy, in dreamings, fond converse can
    share
With my soul's earliest treasure, fair Nelly Adair.

Ye are dear to my bosom, ye green haunts of yore!
'That back to their altar youth's feelings restore,
When beauty's warm spell, round my fond ravish'd
    heart,
Sheds the love-hallow'd incense that ne'er may
    depart.
Away ye gay baubles, proud fortune and fame!
Your grandeur and glory alike I disdain;
Come, fancy—all peerless—with thee let me share
One life-long love-vision with Nelly Adair.

## A LOVE LYRIC.

### AIR—"THE LASS OF ARRANTEENIE."

Now winter's surly reign is o'er,
    The snow has left the mountains;
Fair spring unfolds her vernal store;
    And sunshine gilds the fountains:
Adown the woodland's winding glade,
    My Mary, let us wander,
And share the joys by nature spread,
    In wild, sweet, simple grandeur.

By racing burn and hazel screen
    The April flow'rs are springing,
And song-birds gay thro' every scene
    Their lays of love are singing.

There, far from fashion's faithless show,
    Its cares and fruitless pining,
We'll share love's fond endearing glow,
    Beyond proud wealth's divining.

Let mad ambition climb to pow'r,
    Give pride its tinsell'd grandeur,
Give sordid minds their golden dow'r,
    And fashion halls of splendor ;
Give me Monstuart's leafy grove,
    And thee, my Mary, by me,
To roam at will and talk of love,
    Ev'n monarchs might envy me.

We'll stray till night in starry pride,
    Reveal's its beaming glories ;
Truth-hallow'd love our hearts shall guide,
    And hope dance light before us.
Enfolded to this ardent breast,
    With faith that ne'er can vary,
In pure devotion fondly press'd,
    I'll bless my blue-eyed Mary.

## SIC A WIFE AS WILLIE HAD.

WILLIE Wanless lived on Jed,
    A bickermaker bould and slee,
As greedy as the rav'nous gled,
    And crafty as a fox was he,
He had a wife o' gipsey kin,
A cave-bred carlin' swart and thin :
The neebors ca'd her *cut-the-win ;*
    A kittle dame I trow was she.
CHORUS—"O' sic a wife as Willie had !"
        As Willie had, as Willie had !
        Had horned Belzie been her dad,
        A viler pest she couldna be.

She was a sprout o' spaewife breed,
    That round the borders bore the gree ;
And glamour'd a' the youth o' Tweed,
    Wi' mony a cruel sinfu' lee.
She was the get o' Judith Faa,
They hang'd langsyne on Berwick Law
For stealin' gentle bairns awa,
    To gain a heavy ransom fee.

            O sic a wife, etc.


Her form was tall, her shouthers braid,
    Her black hair matted on her bree,
Her dark een sunken in her head,
    Aye gleamin' fou o' fiendish glee.
She swam the river like an eel ;
The tallest tree like cat she'd speel ;
And ne'er could maukin cross a fell,
    And jouk sae gleg o' limb as she.

            O sic a wife, etc.


At a' the trysts, at a' the fairs,
    Frae Kelso to the banks o' Dee,
She duly trogg'd wi' Willie's wares ;        .
    And dreaded far and near was she.
She wadna cowe for priest or laird—
For gentles she had nae regard,
'Tween belted knight and smutty caird
    Nae difference could the randy see.

            O sic a wife, etc.


For how she fenn'd wi' her guidman,
    It needsna trouble you nor me ;
Nae doots he reckon'd her a swan,
    And she thocht him a hinnie bee !
For tho' they baith gat steamin' fou,
And fought like ither randy crew,

They aye had rowth to fry and stew,
 And meal and maut to mak them gree.
  O sic a wife, etc.

The fattest hens 'tween Tyne and Tweed,
 The brawest bleachings on the lea
They'd stown, wi' siccan dexterous speed,
 As aye defied the tentiest e'e.
If hemm'd to bear her booty aff,
She weel could swing a *Jeddart staff*—
And fell the beagle, like a cauf,
 Wha'd daur to curb her liberty.
  O sic a wife, etc.

Ae day she gae'd to Kelso tryst
 A wauly load o' bickers wi';
The sodgers had come there to list,
 Wi' fife and drum and martial glee,
Wi' mony a wild unhallowed aith,
She swore they'd come her trade to scath;
And bann'd wi' sic disloyal breath,
 She fairly set their craft ajee.
  O sic a wife, etc.

They dragged her to the auld Tolbooth,
 But just as weel they'd let her be—
She charg'd the jailor, claw and tooth,
 And fley'd him till he set her free!
Then doon she bang'd him in the mire,
And lap and leugh wi' vengfu' ire,
Syne set the auld tolbooth on fire,
 And owre the meadows hame did flee!
  O sic a wife, etc.

To Yetholm kirk they raucht her ance,
 Some gospel benison to pree;

She straight began to shout and dance,
   When Bangor woke his haly glee !
Mess John he graned wi' pious dread,
He daur'd na preach—he daur'd na read :
She cuist her bauchels at his head,
    And skipp'd and flang to wild degree !
       O sic a wife, etc.

For civil law or moral rule,
   She didna care a single flea :
The scoff o' branks or cutty stool,
   Just left her as she wont to be.
At length, ae year, some secret fate,
Sent down the famous Hawick spate,
And bore her aff, a wee o'er late,
    To feed the partans in the sea !
       O sic a wife, etc.

## DOWN IN YON WOODLAND.

Down in yon woodland among the green boughs,
By the clear winding river, that sings as it flows,
On a soft mossy bank, where the bluebells are spring-
    ing ;
And the merle its sweet carol to evening is singing ;
A counting the moments though swiftly they flee,
My lov'd one, my true one is waiting for me !
    A counting the moments, etc.

I fancy I hear his fond sigh on the breeze,
As he whispers my name to the flowers and the trees.
And the soft flowing tones of his melody wander,
Thro' every reft scene where the echoes meander ;
Whilst low in yon dell, 'neath the great linden tree,
My lov'd one, my true one is waiting for me.
    Whilst low in yon dell, etc.

The stock dove is calling his mate to his side,
To tell her his love in the calm eventide—
Lo ! scorning all dangers around and above her,
How fondly she speeds to the bow'r of her lover !
Even so would I haste, had I wings such as she,
Where my lov'd one, my true one is waiting for me.
      Even so would I speed, etc.

How feeble—inconstant—how fleeting and cold,
Seems the love that is based on an altar of gold !
O ! shield me ye shades from its lurements forever!
And grant me a cot by this dear rolling river !
My life's love to share 'neath yon green linden tree,
With the lov'd one, the true one that's waiting for me.
      My life's love to share, etc.

## THE SMUT MACHINE.

### AIR—"THE TINKLER'S WEDDING."

ATTEND a' ye whom it concerns,—
A' ye wha' hae got wives and bairns :
An honest miller frae the Mearns
   Has cross'd the sea to be our freen ;
He 's bigg'd a mill in Habbie's hole,
And, tho' it sounds a wee thought droll,
He winna charge a raxin' toll,
   Nor use a filthy smut machine.

CHORUS—O, weary fa' the smut machine,
      The menseless thievin' smut machine;
      Its greedy maw ye ne'er can sta',
      The roguish, rievin' smut machine.

An honest miller ! Farmers a',
Come, cast your grumblin' thrums awa';
'Tho' lang we've grudg' our melders sma',
  And lichter than they should hae been ;
Nae mair guid wives need scauld and greet,
Nor bairns get stinted o' their meat ;
We now can shun the wily cheat,
  The plaguey, pilf'rin smut machine.

CHORUS—O, weary fa' the smut machine, etc.

'The knave who first devised the plan
Could scarce deserve the name o' man ;
His conscience aye 'neath poortiths ban,
  Must many a dolefu' fleg have gien,
For while he cleaned his neighbour's meal,
'Twas plain his ain he meant to steal ;
He could nae gleger serve the de'il,
  'Than make a pilferin smut machine.

CHORUS—O, weary fa' the smut machine, etc.

A miller aye has sonsie hens,
And hogs sae fat they burst their pens,
But what they thrive on nae ane kens ;
  Their rowthiest dish is seldom seen ;
But mony a puir wee hungry chiel
Maun toil around the farmer's fiel,
Sair scrimpit o' his crowdie meal,
  To glut a greedy smut machine.

CHORUS—O, weary fa' the smut machine, etc.

Last spring was backward, cauld and wet,
'The summer dry, and scarthin' het ;
And craps by vermin sae beset,
  'The like o't seldom has been seen ;
Neist cam the hair'st wi' boist'rous brash
And wreck'd our fiel's wi' wild stramash—

We had but little left to thrash,
   Far less to gie a smut machine.
CHORUS—O, weary fa' the smut machine, etc.

For ten lang days my flail I flang,
And thrash'd my sheaves wi' birrfu' bang;
But tho' ilk day was ten hours lang,
   I scarce could make a peck bedeen.
I sent a hunner to the mill,
But, thanks to pawky Meldrum's skill,
Just forty punds came hame to Will,
   The lave went wi' the smut machine.
CHORUS—O, weary fa' the smut machine, etc.

At first I trow'd 'twas some mistak',
Or that some hole was in the sack,
But nae; the eighth comman' was brak,
   And 'twadna mend it to complain,
But rather wad I ply my flail
To thrash the clouds, and eat the hail,
Or feed on browse or sourock kail,
   Than trust a roguish smut machine
CHORUS—O, weary fa' the smut machine, etc.

Fate lang has to our pray'rs been deaf,
Now, Guid be praised, we've got relief;
The knaves that thrive by sic mischief
   Will soon reform, or fast get lean;
When Nature winds up earth's concerns,
And Belzie comes to claim his bairns,
He 'll leave the miller frae the Mearns,
   Because he used nae smut machine.
CHORUS—O, weary fa' the smut machine, etc.

———

M

# I AM SOMEBODY NOO.

AIR—"TODLIN' BUTT AND TODLIN' BEN."

COME hither, my dawtie, and join in my sang;
Ne'er fash how the cauld blasts o' winter may bang,
Let's mak' our hearts blythe o'er what comforts we
        share,
And the langer we leeve aye be lookin' for mair.
I ance was as puir as a frog in a stane;
Scarce och't of the man save the skin and the bane;
I was naebody then, and respeckit by few,
But, praise be to fortune, I'm somebody noo.
CHORUS—I'm somebody noo, I'm somebody noo,
        O praise be to fortune, I'm somebody noo.

I toil'd late and early for mony a year,
For I thocht honest labor wud thrive in the rear,
But the langer I strave aye the puirer I fen'd,
Till povereesed conscience na mair could contend;
She counsell'd me firmly to alter my creed,
And eagerly I to her counsel gave heed;
'Twas lucky I did, lass, as weel you may trow,
For you see I'm leukt up to, as somebody noo.
        As somebody noo, as somebody noo, etc.

I aye had a notion to leuk like a laird,
To ha'e a fine palace and bonnie flow'r yaird,
Wi' rowth o' braw flunkies to rin at my ca',
And a watch dog to scare a' mean vagrants awa';
So I set mysel' out for to cheet and to lee,
And to mak' my companions o' folks that were hie;
I dealt in *lang credits*, and togg'd like a Jew.
And I flatter'd and fawn'd till I'm somebody noo.
        I'm somebody noo, I'm somebody noo, etc.

The lawyer comes here wi' his pate fu' o' skill,
And the doctor attends tho' 'tis no wi' his bill,
The justice, the squire, and his revrence Mess John,
Wi' a britherly kindness our dignity own.
There are few o' our betters upon us leuk doon,
And we'll sune be as hie as the folks in the moon ;
Tho' it teuk some hard grubin' sic heicht to win to,
Gif conscience keeps mum, I am somebody noo.

  I am somebody noo, I am somebody noo, etc.


I neir liked a beggar since e'er I was born,
Wha howffs wi' the humble earns little but scorn,
What matter how honesty seasons his plea,
It's the smile o' my betters brings profit to me.
The man wha in life to position wad rise,
That mean scaur-craw puirtith maun learn to despise,
I've lang held the maxim, and thrave by it too,
Till by aye leuken upwards, I'm somebody noo.

  I'm somebody noo, I'm somebody noo, etc.


Tho' lang, lass, you've yaup'd like a hen in the pook,
You may yet be a duchess, gif I be a duke,
You'll own as braw' triggin' as mony a queen,
In your gilt coach by day, and your sofa at e'en ;
We'll hae fine damask carpets to spread 'neath our
   feet,
And our table sall grane wi' a' dainties that's sweet,
Wi' eggs fried in gravy, and rare chicken stew,
An' a greybeard to croon't, since I'm somebody noo.

  I'm somebody noo, I'm somebody noo, etc.


Tho' neebors may whiles say I'm loopy and vain,
And speel on a ladder that is na my ain,
As lang's I can sprattle still upwards I'll aim,
Gif the Shirras *yell-nowte* dinna fasten his claim.

A wee grip o' greatness may heeze me to mair;
Come honest, come fause, what the diel need we
      care !
It's grand to be great, lass, I trow you'll allow,
Whae'er pays the piper, I'm somebody noo.

    I'm somebody noo, I'm somebody noo,
    Whae'er pays the piper, I'm somebody noo.

## MARY OF STRATHCONNAN.

### AIR—"AFTON WATER."

By Huron's calm tide, when the sun's in the west,
And his rays kiss the wavelets that glide o'er its
    breast,
When the loud choral din of the forest declines,
And the smoke of the hamlet is wreathing the pines,
Strathconnan's green arbors, how dear is their shade,
As eve's ling'ring haloes still gleam through the
    glade,
Where love's tryst I hold 'neath yon sweet linden
    tree,
With Mary, the pride of Strathconnan's green lea.

Tho' humble her life in her rural abode,
Where the stream to the flowers chants it sweet
    fitful ode,
In rustic simplicity's matchless array,
As queen of the sylvans she's throned in my lay :
But wider her empire than song can impart,
I've built her a shrine in the core of my heart,
Where its proudest emotions her homage shall be,
Fair Mary, the pride of Strathconnan's green lea.

O ! had I the treasures of earth's richest zone:
Its mightiest sceptre, its loftiest throne,
With all its high honors and garniture vain,
If shared not with Mary, to me all were pain;
I'd pine from the dawn till the night's darksome tide,
O'er my vision-wreck'd fancy again should preside,
If fate my soul's queen-gift denied her to be,
Fair Mary, the pride of Strathconnan's green lea.

Go, cull me the flower with the blue drooping bell,
That blooms where the water winds down the soft
    dell,
And gather yon rose from its wild thorny spray,
And the violet that gladdens the holm with its ray,
The meak meadow pink with its blushes of love,
And all the chaste flower-gems of valley and grove,
I'll twine them together a garland to be
For Mary, the pride of Strathconnan's green lea.

I woo not the music that swells in proud domes,
Where the soul in a lab'rynth of melody roams,
While the phantoms of fashion in soulless display,
Affectedly breathe forth the meaningless lay,
But give me the strains that are fresh from the heart,
The groves holy cadence, untutored by art,
I'll pour their wild raptures and pure simple glee,
To Mary, the pride of Strathconnan's green lea.

---

## HEY DONALD! HOW DONALD!

The first verse and chorus of the following song are the
fragment of an unfinished song by Robt. Tannahill.

Now summer smiles on bank and brae,
And nature bids the heart be gay,

But, a' the joys o' flow'ry May,
  Wi' pleasure canna move me.
    Hey Donald ! how Donald !
  . Think upon your vow, Donald,
    Mind the heathery knowe, Donald,
    Whar' ye vow'd to love me !

Now lane 's my time since thou'rt awa',
Perchance 'mang fraes, afar, to fa' :
I weary roam by glen and shaw,
  Whar' wild-flow'r wreathes you wove me ;
    Hey Donald ! how Donald, etc,

Ilk gaudy charm o' summer bloom,
Wears to my e'e some lint o' gloom ;
The birdies whistling 'mang the broom
  Wi' painful feelings move me.
    Hey Donald, how Donald, etc.

My mother bids me dicht my e'e,
My faither frets and frowns on me ;
And for that love I've plighted thee,
  They ear' and late reprove me.
    Hey Donald ! how Donald, etc.

They bid me spin, they bid me sing,
They try a' airts my faith to ding ;
They've hid from me thy token ring,
  The pledge you gave to love me.
    Hey Donald ! how Donald, etc.

But wharsoe'er, by land or sea,
My sodger love thy lot may be,
Thy truth shall ne'er be wranged by me,
  I swear by a' above me.
    Hey Donald ! how Donald, etc.

## BRAES O' THE TYNE.

LASSIE, I loe thee, aft hae I tauld the
How dowie my life in thy absence would be,
Close to this bosom again let me fauld thee,
Fondly and truly it beats but for thee ;
Here in the dell, where the birk and the rowan tree
Close wi' the hazel and slaethorn entwine,
While our flocks peacefully graze on the gowan lee,
Dearest ! come niffer thy life plight wi' mine.

Gracefu' and bonnie the wee flow'rs are springing,
Clearly the stream mingles doon thro' the glen ;
The mavis and linwhite are cantily singing ;
The sun's setting halo yet gleams on the ben.
A' the bright joys o' the summer gay flow'ry prime
Roun' our wee love-biel in sweetness shall vie :
Beauty and song mak' our love haunt a bowry clime,
Chaster and purer as e'enin' draws nigh.

Sma' are my riches and lowly my dwellin',
And humble the lot I can proffer to thee ;
Nae title hae I to a proud garnished mailin ;
The tow'rs or the tinsel o' lofty degree.
Down on yon strath, whar the sunlicht sae bonnie
    glows,
Stands my wee cot on the braes o' the Tyne,
Three score and ten—a' my warld's wealth o' bonnie
    yowes :
Lass, can you lo'e me, and a' shall be thine ?

Gaily the lark sings at dawn o'er the shealing,
Waking his love frae the gowansprent lea ;
And a' the fresh joys o' the summer revealing,
Kind nature at noontide shall open for thee ;

And when the e'ening shades ca' hame the roaming
    bee,
Laden wi' sweets to his saft mossy den ;
While the hoarse *ryecraik* is carping his gloamin'
    glee,
Swiftly I'll hie to thee, lassie, again.

Purely our lives, as the tide o' the burnie,
Shall glide like its waters that hum to the flow'rs,
And peace, love and truth, to the end o' our journey,
Far mair than the palace can boast—shall be ours.
Lassie, I lo'e thee—long, long I've sigh'd for thee,
A' this fond heart can gie, love shall be thine,
Want ne'er shall be thy fa'—rowth I'll provide for
    thee ;
Come ! bless my wee cot on the braes o' the Tyne.

## IT'S AN' ILL WIN' THAT BLAWS NAEBODY GOOD.

As I sit by my ingle and smoke at my weed,
While the snawstorm is crakin' the rufe ow're my
    head,
And the cauld wheelin' drift thro' ilk cranny blaws
    ben,
'Till it's piled up and fruize' at the very fire en' ;
I whiles grudge the comforts the wealthy enjoy,
In their warm couthie ha's, free frae care's cauld
    alloy,
'Till conscience cries hooly—indulge na sic mood,
" Its an ill win' that blaws naebody good."

This pithy auld proverb I learn'd in my youth,
And often my solace I fand in its truth :
For e'en when my loss prov'd some ither chiel's gain,
I said—" We hae nocht we can weel ca' our ain."

A conscience that's clear o' the carpins o' crime,
Is the treasures unshaken by tempest or time :
We ne'er can be reft o't—blaw civil or rude,—
" Its an ill win' that blaws naebody good,"

Frae the hour o' our birth till the hour that we dee,
To the great law o'change we aye subject maun be ;
There's nae settled nick whar its wheel may stan'
    still,
It keeps rowin' forever in spite o' our skill :
And aft as we loup at the goal o' our hope,
We tapple and fa' mid disasters to grope,
But the wreck o' one's fa' gies a score aft their food :
" Its an ill win' that blaws naebody good."

Yon Laird has his palace and bonnie estate,
And a dozen mean flunkies his ca' to await,
He has wealth on the lan, he has wealth on the sea,
But wifeless and heirless he's fated to be ;
His friens he discards them—tho' shamefu to tell,
He wants e'en the saul to enjoy it himsel :
That the parish will heir him 'tis weel understood :
" Its an ill win' that blaws naebody good."

The freaks o' dame fortune may puzzle us sair,
Her highways, and byeways, 'tween hope and
    despair ;
Sic uphills and downhills she jogs us thro' life,
Midst brightness and darkness, and concord and
    strife !
Some purpose o' Providence orders it sae,
And tho' whiles our prospect seems blirtie and wae,
We neer should sit down o'er our sorrows to brood :
"Its an ill win' that blaws naebody good."

I aften hae thocht, as I santer'd alane,
To ponder o'er pages o' time that had gane,

How lucky the lot o' some fellows might be,
Had they studied auld Nature's designments like me:
How purely impartial she ettles to rule ;
How nane should be tyrant, and nane should be
    snool,
'Twad save meikle bickerin', and heartbreak, and
    fued :—
" Its an ill win' that blaws naebody good."

Thank heav'n for a biel and wee bit o' soil ;
A head that can think, and a han' that can toil ;
A sonsie kin' spouse and some blythe ruddy bairns,
Wi' the brats and the brose that leal industry earns :
The menseless and fretfu may caption for gear,
And girn at a' blasts that sweep o'er the year :
This saw for my maxim aye tempers my mood :—
" Its an ill win' that blaws naebody good."

## THE WANDERER.

FAR away o'er land and sea, wheresoe'er thy wander-
    ings be,
In quest of fame or fortune, prone apart from me
    to roam ;
Dost thou e'er thou rambler I fancy, that the spirit
    of thy Nancy
    Is with weary watchings, worn and woe,
    'Lorn pining here at home?

While ambition's dazzling star o'er the gory field of
    war
Inspires thy breast to prowess bold thro' danger's
    wild career

Whilst battle's bolts are gleaming and glory's
    pennon streaming,
  Can soft sad thoughts of home and love
  Recal thy spirit here?

In the dewy twilight shade, of the leafy woodland
    glade—
While the ring dove's plaintive murmuring floats
    sweetly on the wind :—
Where the tinkling streamlet gushes 'mongst the
    fragrant flow'rs and bushes,
  Wilt thou e'er thou wanderer meet again
  With her you've left behind?

Oh! that weary bauble gold! what hearts are
    bought and sold
By the bright ensnaring witcheries that sparkle
    round its shrine!
What false, false words are spoken! what fond ties
    rudely broken!
  What chilling anguish preys on breasts
  As prone to trust as mine!

Sweet hope! thy smiles impart to my sadly beating
    heart;
Give visions dear to truth sincere and joy for years
    to come!
When free from bloody danger, from the land of
    foe and stranger,
  Kind peace and honest-hearted love
  Shall call my wanderer home.

# THE SPRING AT THE FOOT OF THE HILL.

By the brink of yon crystaline spring
  That flows at the foot of the hill,
Where the dark-waving cedars to fling
  Their shadows o'er meadow and rill,—
There's a bow'r where the woodbine and wild trail-
    ing vine
In the folds of affection enchantingly twine;
Where far from the city I often recline
  By that spring at the foot of the hill.

When the stillness of ev'ning descends,
  There's a magical test in the air,
Unknown to the discord that blends
  Midst the hum and the bustle of care.
How my fancy delights in that hour,
  To wander along by the rill;
While the zephyr in fragrance is bathing its wing
Midst the wild simple flowers in the valley that
    spring;
And the robin his sweet vesper-carol doth sing
  By the spring at the foot of the hill.

There's a maiden who dwells in the dale—
  A comely fresh flower of the wild;
I saw her one eve' with her pail,
  Which she dipp'd in the fountain and fill'd.
Oh! beauty transcendant! thy spell
  From that moment my bosom did fill;
For the fairest of forms and the sweetest of looks
Ever seen in my visions, or read of in books,
Were hers whom I saw in that Eden of nooks,
  By the spring at the foot of the hill.

How I love of that water to drink !
   From its fountain fresh sparkling amain ;
And oft as I rise from its brink
   I am tempted to taste it again.
In that region the spirit of love
   Doth surely his nectar distil ;
And willing that mortals his relish should prove
Hath scoop'd out that well in the bow'ry alcove,
And bade that fair nymph with the pail often rove
   By the spring at the foot of the hill.

In my soul I have treasured her form,
   So entrancingly artless and fair,
That the city no longer can charm
   With its pomp and its false-fleeting glare.
Away from the din of its crowd,
   Be my lot still to revel at will,
Midst rural delights and serenity blest,
With the maiden whose image is shrined in my
     breast,            [carest,
Oh ! how hallow'd my hours in her fond smiles
   By the spring at the foot of the hill.

---

## THE LOWN GLEN.

### AIR—"JOHN ANDERSON MY JO," OR "GI'E MORRICE."

O, BONNIE is the lown\* glen,
   And calm the gloamin' hour,
And sweetly sings the canty merle
   Abune the hawthorn bow'r ;
The gushin' burn jouks down the brae,
   Amang the brackens green ;
And the bloomin' slaethorn shimmers
   In the pearly dews o' e'en.

---

\* Calm and tranquil.

The purple-pendled foxglove
  Begins to droop its bell,
And the meek wee gowan faulds its e'e,
  To nestle in the dell.
Its creamy flowers, the tanglin' brier
  Weaves 'mang the yellow broom,
And the woodbine's scented tassels hang
  Among the birken bloom.

O l weel I lo'e to wander
  Alang the bickerin' stream,
When love's star o'er the eastern height
  First sheds its haly beam.
When the saft breeze fans the sweet wee flow'rs
  That bank and brae adorn,
And the peace and joy o' nature meet
  Beside the woodland burn.

The lavroc leaves the blue lift,
  Whar high he sang a' day ;
And tauld to heaven and earth his love,—
  For *love* is aye his lay.
In safter cadence flutterin' down,
  Aye mellower sounds his glee,
For, though his spray is on the cloud,
  His love is on the lea.

O l leeze me on this lone glen l
  And a' its winsome spells ;
But chiefly love's dear glamourie,*
  When gloamin' shades the fells.
When my leal lad, wha piped frae dawn
  Upon the mountains' stie, †
Like the tunefu' lavroc hastens down,
  To hald his tryste wi me.

---

* Bewilderment or enchantment.
† Steep.

# I'M NO THE QUEER FALLOW I'VE BEEN

I'M no the queer fallow I've been
 When I livit a bachelor's life,
For since I've been buckled to Jean
 I hae comforts mair couthie and rife—
I've a rowthie bit hame o' my ain,
 A cow and a bonnie kail yard ;
Wi' fouth o' potatoes and grain,
 And can leeve beyont hunger's regard.
   I'm no the queer fallow, etc.

Oh, the climate o' life is but cauld,
 And scanty its blessings, I trow,
To a chiel that's unmarried and auld,
 Nae matter what grists in his pow ;
He's just a puir waif on the wave,
 Adrift on adversity's main :
Till death bangs his bouk i' the grave,
 He's the sport o' mishanter and pain.
   I'm no the queer fallow, etc.

At times when I think on the past,
 I can scarcely win owre wi' the shame,
How I squandèrt my earnins sae fast,
 And had neither a spouse nor a hame ;
How I stammert my way thro' the warl',
 Uncar'd for by a' but myself ;
Sae few will befrein' a puir carle
 When they ken he is scant o' the pelf !
   I'm no the queer fallow, etc.

When single my cleidin was slops,
 And seenil it fitted me weel ;
It was niffered for cheapness in shops,
 Baith thriftless and shabby genteel.

Now ye see by the coat on my back,
   And my breeks that are hodden and new,
That Jean has a hamely bit knack
   O' makin' guid claithing o' woo'.
       I'm no the queer fallow, etc.

It's no that I brag o' my dame,
   But search thro' ilk loop o' the lan',
And ye'll no fin' a biener bit hame,
   Nor a kinder guid wife to her man!
Besides, we've a bonnie lass bairn,
   That I prize like the licht o' my e'e :
It gies strength tho' I'm toil'd and forfairn,
   When she laughs and cries, " Daddy," to me.
       I'm no the queer fallow, etc.

It was proven langsyne i' the warl'—
   There's nane daur dispute it ava—
(I carena tho' cynics may snarl)
   That wedlock is nature's prime law.
It's the pith and the standard o' man—
   Society's haliest tie ;
And he's under society's ban
   That feels nae as happy as I.
       I'm no the queer fallow, etc.

## JEANIE LOWE.

I LOV'D a pretty maiden,
   When my life was young and gay,
When my locks were dark, and smooth my face—
   In a land far, far away !
When my march was o'er the mountain steep !
   Like the roving summer wind,
And my home was down in the valley deep,
   Where the birch and bramble twined.

I lov'd a pretty maiden :
   And her name was Jeanie Lowe ;
But I cannot sing, with the fire of youth,
   Of her peerless beauty now !
I only glean from memory's forms,
   O'er life's far checquered waste,
A tithe of its weird and winning charms,
   Still sacred to my breast.

I lov'd that pretty maiden,
   But why I cannot tell—
'Twas not because her graceful form
   Did others far excel !
'Twas not because her golden hair
   In sunshine deck't her brow !
That her eyes were blue and face was fair,
   That I lov'd young Jeanie Lowe !

I lov'd that pretty maiden
   With a love more pure and strong
Than e'er was nurs'd in mute despair,
   Or breath'd in joyous song !
'Twas love—but not of that earthly kind
   That turns so sere and cold,
As time's rife changes warp the mind,
   And hearts, and their hopes turn old.

I lov'd that pretty maiden ;
   And 1 feel that I love her now :
Though her eyes, like mine, be dimm'd by age,
   And its forrows on her brow !
Though slow in pace, and frail in frame,
   She bows to the blast of time !
To my fancy's eye, she seems the same
   I lov'd, in her life's young prime.

I left her, one sad morning :—
   Her eyes like mine were dry :
   N

But we little thought what dreary years
   Should part us, till we'd die !
We little dream'd that rash farewell
   Should wring our memories now ;
Or my jarring harpstrings wake to tell
   Of my long-lost Jeanie Lowe.

## MY AULD FIDDLE.

AYE, that's my auld fiddle that hangs in the neuk :
And my heart whiles feels dowie when on it I look ;
Sae mony auld mem'ries and sympathies rise,
Frae the mist o' past years wi' their griefs and their
   joys.
'Twas far far away, owre the braid foamin' main,
In a land whar my feet ne'er may travel again ;
In the land o' brave hearts—in the days o' langsyne,
Where I first learned to tune that auld fiddle o'
   mine.

I then was a laddie untramel'd by care,
Wi' a spirit as free as my ain mountain air ;
A bosom wi' hamely affections imbued,
And a sprinkling o' social desire in my blood ;
I played to the bairns in the calm summer e'en,
As they frisked wi' delight on the lown village
   green,
'Till the auld folk wad aft wi' the younkers combine,
And skip to that couthie auld fiddle o' mine.

I've tuned in bothies 'mang swains and their jo's,
'Till they cuist aff their hobnails and spankt in their
   hose !             [the reel,
"Till they whirl'd in the jig, and they dash'd through
Cut high upon tiptae, and stamped wi' the heel !

While rafter and ruiftree, and e'en the stain wa',
Or concord or discord, aft threatened to fa' ;
And down ilk brown cheek stream'd the warm
    sweaty brine,
As they bobb'd to that canty auld fiddle o' mine.

In the farmer's blyth spence, in the baron's proud
    hall,
At kirn, and at bridal, and holiday ball,
Nae guest o' the party, nor humble nor high,
Could brag o' a kindlier reception than I ;
For my mellow-voiced fiddle had magic they said,
And the wale o' their feast was the music it made ;
The sangs aye grew sweeter—the dancin' mair fine,
When led by that dainty auld fiddle o' mine.

I've waked its sweet spirit on land and on sea !
I've tuned it to sorrow, 'Ive tuned it to glee,
I've screwed up its strings to the cadence o' love,—
To the thrill o' the lavroc—the wail o' the dove !
I've raised its bauld tones to the patriot's lay
In the clime o' my birth, and in climes far away :
And many memorials o' hallow'd langsyne,
Are wreathed roun' that friendly auld fiddle o' mine.

"Twas the gift o' a cronie, true-hearted and leal,
And he taught me the method to play on't as weel ;
Thro' guid and ill-fortune it's aye been my plea,
'That nae proffer could wile the auld keepsake frae
    me ;
'Tho' many the jostles and flegs we hae gat—
We are baith o' us Scotch and the better for that ;
So as lang as I'm leevin' I'll never resign,
That long-treasured faithfu' auld fiddle o' mine.

## THE CLACKITT STREET COO.

### BY A CLACKITT STREET POLICEMAN.

PERHAPS ye'll hae heard o' the Clackitt street coo;
If no ye've a chance for to hear o' her noo :
Nae cow in the loanin wi' her could compare,
Sae rowth was her milk and its virtues sae rare!
The brute grew sae famous, that gang whar ye micht,
Frae the grey dawn o' morn till the mirk hour o'
 nicht,
The theme o' ilk gossip the neighbourhood thro',
Was aye sure to turn on the Clackitt street coo.

'Twas said, by some crone wha' pretended to skill,
That her milk was a cure for amaist every ill,
And folk that were simple and eithly deceived,
The wonderfu statement as deftly believed !
They a' ran to buy it wi' credulous haste,
When ony mishanter their health wad molest,
Till the craft o' the doctor a failure sune grew,
Thro' the wonderfu' milk o' the Clackitt street coo!

Besides, it had ither peculiar charms
Which I 'll strive to rehearse in poetical terms :
'Twas said that auld spinsters, and bachelors too,
By drinkin' o't freely, their youth could renew !
That it banish'd the freckles and furrows o' time !
Restored a' the ardour and hues o' life's prime !
Made wedlock aye certain, and spouses aye true,
The wonderfu' milk o' the Clackitt street coo !

Gif a lassie were dwarfish, ill-featured and dun,
And nae Jo's affections were likely to win ;
Gif she ettled the han o' some chiel to attain,
And plied a' her force o' attractions in vain ;

'Though big as a giant and proud as a duke,
As firm as a gudgeon he'd stick on her hook,
Gif she in his tea but ae thimblefu' threw
O' the wonderfu' milk o' the Clackitt street coo !

The Templars wha never encourage a vice,
On their meeting-nights quaff'd it, and vow'd it was
    nice ;
It serv'd them to fang Ideality's spring,
Made fluent their tongues, and inspired them to sing !
It strengthened their lungs, and it mellow'd their
    throats,
'Till their cadence outrivall'd the bleating of goats ;
And fifty mair virtues, forbye these I trow,
They found in the milk o' the Clackitt street coo.

The milliner used it for starchin' her frills—
The apothecar' used it to glozen his pills !
The minister quaffed it to help him to preach !
The dominie drank o't to help him to teach !
His soiled paper collars he spung'd wi't, they say,
For the lad was too frugal to throw them away—
And shampoon'd his ringlets—as some folks allow,
Wi' the rich creamy milk o' the Clackitt street coo.

Be't fact or be't fable—I've heard too of late,
O' a laird and his lady, o' heirless estate,
Wha advised by the spaewife, ae eeni'n stepp'd owre,
Resolved for to test its miraculous power !
They drank o't wi' freedom and syne slippit hame—
And in nine short months after just wot ye what
    came ;
Ye may guess 'twas an heir—but I tell ye 'twas two,
'Thro' the wonderfu' milk o' the Clackitt street coo.

Nae doubt o't—a coo o' sic virtues as she,
Wad sune turn a mark for ilk covetous e'e :

Nae wonder gif envy in friendly disguise
Soon fell on a project to seize sic a prize!
They slandered the owner and glamour'd his wife,
And bred sic a storm o' connubial strife,
As a' their domestic arrangments o'erthrew,
Resolv'd to get haud o' the Clackitt street coo!

At length—to evade a bit crook in the law,
She was made a mock sale o' to Eppie McCraw,
Wha teuk the de'il's coonsel her conscience to hush—
That "*a bird in the han' was worth twa in the bush.*"
Quo' she—"here nae langer in puirtith I'll grane,
This coo 's just as gude's the philosopher's stane,
On the strength o' her milk and her butter, I trow,
I'll sune speel to wealth wi' the Clackitt street coo."

But the loftiest castle we bigg in the air,
However sae strang and however sae fair—
The first sweeping surge o' adversity's storm,
To the chaos o' vapours will scatter its form!
Sae fared the grand structure o' Eppie McCraw,
Deceitfully based on her neebour's doonfa :—
May honour aye cling just whar honour is due,
And the right owner hae the Clackitt street coo.

------

## SYMPTOMS OF GOOD WEATHER.

STERN winter, inclement and tardy,
    Is off to his boreal home ;
And spring has come forth in her beauty,
    Thro' meadow and woodland to roam ;
The ice-spell is broke from the fountains,
    How gladsome their freedom they sing !

Oh! who would not join in their anthems,
　To welcome the advent of spring?

The gnats o'er the marshes are buzzing,
　They 're playing at April fools!
And the bullfrogs in ecstacy babbling,
　Hold carnival tide in the pools;
O'er the greensward, the lambkins are frisking,
　The partridges drum in the brake,
The catkins are silvering the willows,
　And bees from their torpor awake.

The blue bird is shouting his rapture,
　The cushat is wooing his bride,
And the heron sits watching the troutlets
　As thro' the clear water they glide,
The grasshopper chants 'mong the stubble,
　The walls with the cricket resound;
And the tone of the humming bird's bugle,
　Comes pleasantly floating around.

The ploughman is turning his furrows,
　So gladsome he whistles or sings;
And the zephyrs each other are chasing,
　With music of joy on their wings;
The leaves of the forest are budding,
　The mavis is piping his lay,
And the dewdrops are brilliantly twinkling
　Like opals on every spray.

The sunbeams in sparkling grandeur,
　Are shedding the holiest gleams;
And the lovely, fresh features of nature
　Are mirror'd again in the streams:
The fields are resuming their verdure,
　The snow-drops and lillies appear,
And the daisies have opened their petals
　To gem the young breast of the year.

Oh ! how sweet are the spring's ruddy glories,
    What melody reigns in her voice ;
As she breathes o'er the earth's teeming bosom,
    And bids her pure spirits rejoice !
Like the visions of hope in life's morning,
    In promise so holily pure,
Unsoiled by adversity's blightings ;
    Oh ! would they could always endure.

## LONG AGO.

"Long ago "—those are the words that in hours of
    reflection,
    The sweetest or saddest remembrance impart ;
The beams of delight, or the clouds of dejection,
    With all the emotions that spring in the heart.
When Memory, with hermit devotion, retraces
    The paths we have trod on life's journey below,
Say,—where beats the heart that not only confesses
    A soul-binding spell in the words—"Long ago?"

Long ago was the time when paternal affection
    First moulded our natures to feelings of love,
When with Virtue's reward, or with Vice's correc-
    tion,
    The dawn-dreams of childhood were all interwove.
When the young eye of hope, thro' the gay future
    peering,
    Saw peace, love, and beauty, untainted by woe;
As away on delight's glancing wavelets careering,
    The heart's proudest joys we have shared long
    ago.

Long ago! when our footsteps by woodland or
    mountain,
Pursued the swift flight of the song-bird or bee,
Or strolled by the banks of some clear native foun-
    tain
    That sang on it's course through the green rushy
    lea,
With the song of the lark, to the cloudlet's ascending,
    The balm of the flowers that around us did blow,
In harmony, perfume and beauty all blending,
    No Eden seemed sweeter than our's long ago.

Long ago! who but minds the enraptured emotion
    That stirred the fond breast in love's first glow-
    ing kiss?
As heart pressed to heart, in its ardent devotion,
    Revealed by its throbbings the depth of its bliss,
Tho' the fell breath of falsehood hope's garland
    hath blighted,
    And wreathed in its stead the dark cypress of
    woe,—
As we mourn over vows that too rashly were plighted,
    Don't they still bind our souls to the sweet long
    ago?

Even now—tho' the breast in the toils of ambition
    May pant for the future—it's gifts or it's praise;
As we seek from our cares a brief moment's re-
    mission,
    How sure retrospection her curtain must raise!
Away! ye who Lethe's dark waters preferring,
    Your vices in shades of oblivion would throw;
Oh! give me remembrance, thy fountain, unsparing,
    The bliss-hallowed waves of the sweet long ago.

## MY AIN LAND.

AIR—"JOHN ANDERSON MY JO."

I WADNA gie my ain land for many lands I've seen,
Although they may hae hills as high, and vales as
    fresh and green ;
Tho' history's page, and minstrel's sang, may reach
    them high to fame,   ·
I canna loe them wi' sich pride, nor count them as
    my hame.

There's something in my ain land that nowhere else
    is found,
A holier charm by far than e'er by ither lands was
    own'd,—
It twined like music round my heart, in childhood's
    march sublime,
And still it stirs its loftiest joys, unmarr'd by chance
    or time.

I dearly lo'e my ain land, altho' its far awa,
Tho' rugged are its mountain steeps, and clad in
    June wi' snaw;
Tho' snell its Norland tempests rage, and white its
    torrents foam,
The grandeur o' its wild free spells can charm
    where'er I roam.

The waves that gird my ain land, and lave its rocky
    coast,
Have many a strang invader's bones aneath their
    surges toss't;
And many a cave in nameless glen, where history
    scarce can pry,
Has echoed back the foeman's wail in ages lang
    gone by.

There's wealth within my ain land nae mines of
    goud excel,—
A wealth marauder ne'er could reave, nor wily
    traitor sell;
The Hero's mound, the Martyr's grave, and Truth's
    enduring shrine,
Where bravery, faith, and moral worth their lasting
    proofs combine.

Ye winds that fan my ain land, and o'er the ocean
    sweep,
Oh! waft to soothe a wanderer's mind, some
    whisperings o'er the deep;
Come laden wi' the sacred strains which patriot's
    chaunt wi' pride,
And incense frae yon stern auld hills where nane
    but freemen bide.

## WILL O' THE WOOD.

Thro' the wide forest the zephyrs o' simmer
    Roam, fraught wi' the cadence o' Nature's gay
      sang,
And the eye-beams o' May thro' the green leaflets
    glimmer,
    Or sport wi' delight the tall shadows amang.
Beautiful flowers through the pathway are peering,
    Like pearl-gems at random neglectfully strew'd,
In meek decorations sae artless endearing,
    The sylvan retirement o' Will o' the Wood.

See whar yon cot, frae its bowery seclusion,
    Peeps forth frae its archway o' boughs wavin'
      green ;

Half seemin' to hide frae the warl's pert intrusion,
　　Nae proud sculptured emblems enrichen the
　　　　scene,
But peace, love, and virtue, the purest o' treasures,
　　Wi' health and content's holy blessings imbued,
Endorseth the beauty, enhanceth the pleasures,
　　Ennobleth the dwellin' o' Will o' the Wood.

Tho' simple the structure o' Will's habitation,
　　And few are the fields o' his earthly domain,
Cauld penury ne'er hauds his heart in prostration,—
　　He sings as he toils, and he toils not in vain.
He shares wi' the needy the fruits o' his labour,
　　And ne'er to the wayfaring outcast is rude;
A warm-feeling friend, and a kind honest neighbo'r,
　　Wi' merits untauld is leal Will o' the Wood.

The minion o' pride in his stey chiselled palace,
　　May scan the low cottage o' Will wi' disdain,
While slave to his passions, mean, sordid, and
　　　　jealous,
　　His pomp and his pastime how futile and vain!
Flush'd vice 'mang the faulds o' voluptuous grandeur,
　　The barb o' remorse there by fits may elude,
May gambol wi' wantonness, revel in splendor,—
　　Life's joys are endurin' wi' Will o' the Wood.

----

## LOVE'S CONFIDENCE.

My heart is on the waves to-night, far, far away at
　　sea,
Where, like the sea-gull on its flight, my Harry's
　　bark scuds free;

Where boundless skies in starry sheen o'erarch the
    waters blue,
And orbs, that ne'er on land are seen, rise hourly
    on his view.

Methinks I hear the rushing gales that charm the
    weary tars,
That tautly fill the ample sails, and bend the
    lofty spars.
The cherish'd hum of ditties gay, which watchmen
    on the deep
Oft sing, to while dull time away, whilst weary mess-
    mates sleep.

My Harry's firm and measured pace along the deck
    I hear;
I note his call to man each brace, and tell what
    course to steer,
And swift as forth the dolphin hastes, the stately
    vessel hies,
Till ocean's dark and briny wastes in silvery furrows
    rise.

May every power that favours love, and tends its
    due reward,
In steady vigil wait above, my sailor's life to
    guard ;
From crested rocks, that hidden cower in ambush
    'neath the wave,
From adverse storms, and lightning's power, his
    gallant vessel save.

My Harry's practis'd eye can scan all dangers near
    or far;
He never shrinks from duty's van, in tempest nor
    in war ;

In shipwreck as in battle prone, no laggard coward
    he ;
And while his heart is bravery's throne, it teems
    with love for me.

My heart is on the waves to-night, and if I wake
    or sleep
His manly form shall fill my sight, far straining o'er
    the deep ;
I'll watch þy day each distant sail, that rises o'er
    the main,
And pray to every favoring gale that wafts him
    home again.

www.ingramcontent.com/pod-product-compliance
Lightning Source LLC
Chambersburg PA
CBHW030542040726
47497CB00008B/2551